ADVENTURES WITH ATHENS

A Global Quest

KEM ARFARAS

Special Dedication

Thank you, God for giving me the confidence to believe in myself and for turning my book into a reality. And to my son Athens for being the inspiration to all my stories, my mom for believing and investing in me. To my husband for his time and faithfulness of 35 years. To my precious four grandchildren who are the animal characters in the story, along with two lovely girls—Annabelle and Savannah Greenman for their added inspiration and love in my life.

adventureswithathens1@gmail.com

www.adventureswithathens.com

Prologue

Come along for an epic quest that begins in Athens, Greece and travel the world through secret portals to all seven continents in seven days.

Do you love adventure, mysteries and discovering new things?

Meet Athens and Abigail, who are best friends that have the same dream and are sent on a special quest to fulfill their destiny. Seek out hidden treasures and ancient relics in hopes of discovering six sacred pieces of armor that were crafted in the heavenly realms before their time. Find out how Athens and Abigail make new friends and overcome their fears along the way.

Is your name written in the Lamb's Book of life?

Uncover evil forces that lurk in the shadows of the unforeseen places of the earth. Boldly stand before the gods and kings of past and present in search of Truth. Who is the true King of Kings? It's believed that The Kingdom of Heaven is where the streets are perfected with gold. Does such a kingdom really exist? Will they fulfill their quest in time for the royal banquet and be crowned heirs to the King's throne? Or will they fall into a black hole for all eternity?

Learn about natural phenomena around the world as you dive into this wonderful book and discover things you never knew existed!

Table of Contents

1. The God of All Gods.. 1

2. Who is the Righteous One? 26

3. A Leap of Faith.. 43

4. Conquering Your Fears.. 58

5. Defeating the Enemy... 78

6. A Strange and Unusual Phenomenon 102

7. The King's Mansion 118

Armor of God—Life Application.............................. 144

Full Armor Verses.. 156

Fun Facts.. 158

My God Who is He 175

Missions Around the World....................................... 176

About the Author 180

The World

CHAPTER 1

The God of All Gods

BELT OF TRUTH

Athens, Greece

Staring up at the stars attached to his ceiling, Athens struggled to fall asleep. He could hear the wind blowing outside as the tree branches brushed against his window.

When he sat up to turn off his moon lamp, an old, worn copy of *The Chronicles of Narnia* slipped off the bed and landed on the floor with a quiet thump. As he leaned over the bed to pick it up, a strange sensation traveled through his body.

He gazed at the objects sitting on his dresser: A lion and lamb figurine, a shofar horn, a unique rock collection, and his holy oils from Israel.

Sliding under the covers, he tossed and turned before finally shutting his eyes. Suddenly, Athens was swept away into a dream... or was it a vision? He saw himself standing in an open valley at night.

His eyes widened as he looked up toward the dark sky; a burst of shooting stars fell from heaven and crashed down to Earth.

"What should we do?" whispered Athens' friend, Abigail, who was standing beside him.

Athens was about to ask what his best friend was doing beside him, when a shattering noise thundered from above. A seven-headed, ten-horned great red dragon broke through the darkness, breathing fire as it spanned over their heads. The creature swooped down and opened its mouth, snapping its jagged teeth at them.

"Get down!" Athens grabbed Abigail's wrist and pulled her into a little crevice between a cluster of boulders. The dragon swept back up into the air and began circling above. Abigail trembled with fear.

Deep within him, Athens felt a voice telling him not to move. *"God?"* Athens thought to himself. Sweat trickled down his back as he fought the urge to flee.

Thunder boomed, shaking the earth, followed by a bright flash of lightning, then twelve legions of angels appeared in the sky. Their wings were filled with eyes like that of great eagles and each was armed with weapons forged in the heavenly realm. Seven of them carried bowls of wrath.

"Athens, you and Abigail must listen to me." The voice spoke again, but this time coming from above. *"I have chosen you to carry out a great quest to find the Truth. The truth about the kings of old, the truth about which King reigns supreme, and the truth about who I Am and why I'm here."*

God wanted him? A fourteen-year-old from earth? He had never even left Greece before or traveled without his parents.

"Your mission is to collect six sacred armor pieces that were forged in Heaven, and learn their purposes. These pieces can defend you against all the forces of evil in the world. Each armor piece has a unique function; but together, they can conquer the devil and all of his hosts."

Athens swallowed hard and glanced at Abigail, who was still afraid from her encounter with the dragon and angels. She bit her nails so hard they began to bleed.

"You have six days to find the six armor pieces and deliver them to King Elohim's mansion by the final hour of the seventh day."

The voice paused for a moment before continuing. *"Once all the pieces are retrieved and delivered to King Elohim's mansion, you will become heirs to His throne and receive a great inheritance."* The voice became graver. *"But take heed... there will be great challenges on this journey. However, I have given you the power to overcome them if you obey my voice."*

The blood rushed from Athens' face. "But how ...," he started to ask, when a sound of trumpets blared and grew louder and louder as the world around him slowly vanished.

He opened his eyes upon the last trumpet blast. Sunshine poured in through his bedroom window. His heart pounded hard in his chest. What had the dream meant?

Two swords and a shield that Athens had forged with his own hands hung on his wall across the room, and beside them was a map. The compass on the corner of the map began spinning.

Athens jumped out of bed and ran across the room to study the map; as he approached the map, the compass stopped and pointed right at him.

Three loud knocks rapped on the front door. *Who would be here so early in the morning?* He wondered as he dashed downstairs and flung the door open. He saw that it was his best friend.

Abigail hurried inside the foyer, clutching a thick leather-bound book. Athens closed the door as Abigail opened the book and handed it to him. "I have to show you something." She pointed to a beautifully handwritten note inside the book.

"*Your journey begins on the hilltop of the Acropolis. There you will discover the Unknown God among the other gods and goddesses of the ancients. Then you will go to Egypt in Africa, where you will search for the Breastplate of Righteousness; then to Australia, not far from the Great Barrier Reef, where you'll search for the Gospel Shoes of Peace; next, is Brazil in South America, for the Shield of Faith; then to Antarctica's Deception Island, where the Helmet of Salvation must be found; followed by California's Yosemite National Park in North America, where you will search for the Sword of the Spirit; and finally, to Israel in Asia, where you will meet your destiny. Every country is filled with its own mysteries and hidden treasures waiting to be uncovered. Israel has been set apart as the greatest of them all.*

If you collect and discover what all six armor pieces are used for and achieve the quest, then your dream will come to pass. King Elohim's mansions are made of gold with precious stones and jewels. Even the streets are made of pure gold. You will become great warriors and appointed heirs to His Mighty Kingdom for all eternity. Once you fulfill your destiny, there will be a grand celebration and a royal banquet that will last for seven magnificent years. You will truly be blessed beyond measure if you survive the journey and make it through all seven continents in time." Athens almost dropped the book. "Where did you get this?" he asked.

"I had a strange dream last night, and you were actually in it. When I woke up, this book and note were beside my bed."

Athens scratched his head. "I'm beginning to think this wasn't just a dream. Maybe we really are meant to go on this quest."

Mrs. Arfaras walked into the room. "What are you two doing?"

Athens rubbed his temples.

"Mom, you're not going to believe this, but I had the most incredible dream, and Abigail was in it."

"Yeah," Abigail said, "and he was in my dream too."

"What was your dream about?" Mrs. Arfaras asked.

"I dreamed I was in the presence of God," he said. "He called me by name to seek out six sacred pieces of armor from each continent around the world.

I must learn what each armor piece is used for before I can inherit the King's promise. The only way to enter is by discovering who the True King is and why He was chosen to reign over all the others." Athens leaned against the doorway. "Abigail and I will navigate through the

5

continents; beginning here in Europe, at the Acropolis in our great city of Greece where the images of the gods are kept. I don't know how I'll approach Dad with this mission; I know how he feels about traveling. But if God wants me to go, then He is going to have to make it happen." He opened the French doors leading outside. Elegant vines grew up the pillars on the patio. A cool breeze blew in and caused the vines to shimmer and shine.

"You know your father doesn't like traveling," his mother said, "and now you want to venture across the continents? Your father and I will have to talk about this. Your father got up before sunrise to get an early start in the olive orchard. He said he needed your help today to press the olives." Mrs. Arfaras stepped out onto the patio, which overlooked their backyard filled with olive trees. Barrels of olives were lying everywhere one was sitting next to Mr. Arfaras as he prepped them for the press. She lifted her eyes and the Acropolis came into view; it was sitting on a hilltop afar off. Athens and Abigail walked over to a window to gaze upon it also.

"Thousands of years ago, the renowned kings and queens of ancient Greece lived luxurious lives and had immense wealth. They ruled their kingdoms and built temples to worship their gods. Such kingdoms have risen and fallen over the centuries, and all that remains of them are stone monuments and hoarded treasures. Rumor has it, their spirits still live and roam the earth to this very day," said Mrs. Arfaras.

"Who do you think the King of kings is?" Abigail asked.

"I'm not sure but we are going to find out," Athens responded.

"Do you know how you got your name, Athens?" his mom asked.

Athens shook his head while clutching the book under his arm.

"Well, then let me tell you." She went back inside the house and they followed and stopped in front of Athens' baby picture hanging on the wall.

"Names are very important," Abigail added. "In Hebrew my name means *'my father's joy'*; my last name is Kyriacos, which means *'of the Lord'* in Greek."

"You have a beautiful name, Abigail," said Mrs. Arfaras; then, turned her attention back toward Athens, and stated, "I've never told anyone this before, but I prayed and fasted for three whole days as I asked God to bless us with another beautiful baby. After patiently waiting, I finally got my answer. One day, while visiting the city, I stood on our hotel's rooftop with your brother, sister, and father. The rooftop overlooked the entire city and the ancient ruins of the Acropolis; while we were admiring the view, I started thinking about what we should name you. Your sister came up with the idea of naming you after the great City... Athens. As we pondered the idea, it became clear that this would be a great name for you. We didn't know it at the time, but your name is related to wisdom, war, and crafts. Your middle name is Seth which means *a promise renewed*—so, you're quite unique." She ruffled his hair. "Whenever we would visit local shops before you were born, the shop workers would give me little trinkets that where tokens of honor because they wanted to bless the new baby to come. After your birth we dedicated you to the Lord. We promised God that we would raise you to glorify His great name. Now, here you are, preparing for this global quest. We were going to wait until your birthday to give you a special gift. But since it's so close to your birthday, I'd like to give it to you today. Plus, you'll need it for your journey."

"What is it?" Athens asked.

"It's a surprise. You'll have to wait until your father approves of this quest first, but I promise you're going love it!"

"Ugh. I don't know if I can do this. What if I fail?" Athens' shoulders drooped. He placed the book on an end table.

"You're not going to fail," his mom said. "First, you must have faith, believe in yourself, and trust that God will guide you. Start thinking and acting as if you've already accomplished it, like a true prince." Mrs. Arfaras stretched out her arms and motioned for them to draw near. "Come," they joined hands and she led them in prayer. "Heavenly Father, thank you for allowing us to come before You with our requests. You are the Alpha and Omega, the Beginning, and the End! You are an amazing Father and friend. Please protect my son and Abigail on this quest. I have faith, and I believe in You. They're Yours before they're mine. Their hearts are faithful, ready, and willing to serve. Give them the strength, hope, and courage needed to complete this task. We also pray that You soften Mr. Arfaras' heart. Please help him get rid of any worry, doubt, and fear. Thank You for all You've done, for all You are doing, and for all that is yet to come. It's in Your mighty name we pray, Amen."

His mom sighed. "I need to know that God is with you and that His angels are protecting you, so I won't worry so much while you're on your mission. Let's hope your father will allow it." Mrs. Arfaras walked into the study room to be alone.

The front door closed behind Abigail as she dashed home to speak to her grandmother. Athens ran up to his room carrying the leather-bound book.

He looked into the mirror on the back of his bedroom door; gazing into his deep green eyes, olive complexion, and rich, wavy hair, he imagined how he would look standing next to the King wearing a regal robe and a gold signet ring, complete with a crown of victory upon his head.

But wait, what would my father say? Please, God, let my dad approve of this journey. I need to know who you really are.

Athens turned around and glanced out the window. Just beyond the olive trees and herb garden, the Acropolis sat on the peak of the hill overlooking the city. *Yes, indeed, that's where we'll begin.* His eyes peered down, and out of the corner of his eye he saw his father standing beneath one of the olive trees plucking an olive from its branch. Athens felt compelled to go out and talk to him.

Mrs. Arfaras returned to the kitchen to prepare breakfast. "I'm going to go talk to dad now," Athens said as he headed out the back door. Mrs. Arfaras caught a glimpse of him as he turned the corner. By the time he got outside, Mr. Arfaras was no longer standing under the olive tree.

Athens figured he must have gone down into the cellar with the olive barrels. Athens paced himself as he crept down the stairwell.

Sure enough, he found his dad sitting on an old wooden stool made from one of the barrels. Athens slowly approached him. When his dad looked up he could see a peaceful glow on his face. There was a gentleness about him Athens had never seen before. He knew something unusual must have happened but didn't know what it was.

He looked into his father's light green eyes. "Dad, I have something to tell you."

"And I have something to tell you, too. But you go first," Mr. Arfaras insisted.

Athens leaned on the olive press and stirred the olives that were inside one of the barrels.

"I had an encounter with God in my dream. He's called me on a global quest to seek out the Truth and fulfill my destiny.

"Yes, I know this to be true. An angel of the Lord visited me earlier this morning while I was in the orchard picking olives."

Athens let out a sigh of relief. This was surely an act of God. His dad never would have allowed him to travel across the continents alone without a divine appointment.

"God's quest for your life is a great one. If you don't want to go, I'll understand. Things can get difficult out there, even for a brave and daring young man like yourself. However, there could be great consequences if you choose not to go, because He has already called you to it," his dad stated.

"I understand. I'm honored that He has chosen me for such a time as this. I'll do my best not to let you or Him down." Athens squeezed his dad's shoulder and smiled.

Mrs. Arfaras stepped into the room. She looked at the old, dusty, wooden shelves on the wall behind their heads and noticed numerous jars. Some were filled with olive oil or olives, and some were empty. "Wow, you've been busy down here.

Are you guys hungry? It's time for breakfast," Mrs. Arfaras said. Athens licked his lips and smiled.

"Mom, dad has agreed to let me go on God's quest!" he exclaimed. Then Mrs. Arfaras looked at them and said, "Well, I guess there's only one thing left for me to do. I'll be right back." She ran out of the cellar and into the house, scurrying up the stairs, then back down again and returned to the cellar. She secretly held a lovely, wrapped gift behind her back. "Close your eyes and no peeking." She said as she placed the gift into Athens' hands. He wondered what it could be.

"Okay, open your eyes!" she said.

Before he looked down at the gift, he met her gaze.

Tears of joy and sorrow streamed down his mother's cheeks, so he asked, "Why are you crying, Mom?"

"I can't believe you're going on a quest. It seems like yesterday that you were just a little boy. I'm going to miss you. I'm so honored to call you, my son," she said wiping away her tears.

Athens smiled and looked away, not wanting to get choked up himself. He couldn't help but turn his eyes toward his gift. It felt round and hard. "Go ahead and open it," said Mr. Arfaras. Peeling away the wrapping paper was like opening a window into heaven.

Athens' eyes brightened as he saw an extraordinary onyx globe gleaming in his hands. He rotated it around and around, viewing it from every angle.

The brilliant gemstones which lay in the globe were astonishing. Each precious stone had been carefully selected from around the world and hand-cut into the shapes of the seven continents; Each trimmed with gold. "Wow. This is amazing!"

He stared deep into the globe as it was glowing when rays of light suddenly radiated from it. The colored stones beamed in every direction, filling the entire room.

A vision of heaven appeared above their heads like a golden aura of glory. Athens' mouth hung open in awe.

Mr. Arfaras was mesmerized. "Now, you definitely have something to look forward to. I can hardly believe my eyes."

"I guess the olives will just have to wait," said Mr. Arfaras.

"Your destiny lays before you," said Mrs. Arfaras as they made their way back inside the house.

Three knocks wrapped on the front door. This time Athens knew it would be Abigail.

"Your back just in time for breakfast." Athens said.

"Yum I can't wait, thank you!" Abigail said as she sat down at their table. Mrs. Arfaras served a delicious hot omelet, with a side of berries. After breakfast, Athens ran to his room and grabbed his backpack. He wrapped his globe in a white cloth and placed it inside, leaving the book on his bed.

***

Upon arriving at the bottom of the hill, they stood at the steps leading up to the Acropolis. Athens' mother anointed their heads with frankincense and myrrh oils, and then his father led them in a prayer asking God to bless them, protect them, and give them the wisdom necessary for their journey.

Then, Mr. and Mrs. Arfaras hugged them and waved goodbye. "Athens," Mrs. Arfaras called, as she quickly ran over to him. "Remember to keep your promise to God, keep your secret hidden until the appointed time." She hugged him one last time, then turned and took in a deep breath as she watched them climb the stairs to the top of the Acropolis. Mr. Arfaras sighed.

Abigail gave Athens a curious look but didn't ask. She figured he would tell her when the time was right.

Athens was excited about their journey and was glad that Abigail was called to the task to go along with him. But he was saddened at the thought of not knowing when or if he'd ever see his parents again. Athens felt drawn to walk toward the circle of gods, when a white light flashed before his eyes. A beautiful, angelic being appeared before them; her face was glowing as bright as a star, her eyes were glistening blue, her hair was golden blonde, and her gown shimmered in the light. "Athens, you're here. I've been waiting for you."

"Wait, what?" A million questions raced through his mind, but he asked only one. "Who are you?" he stuttered.

"Do you want to know the Truth, or shall I make something up for you?"

"The Truth, of course," Athens said.

"What do you mean by the Truth?" asked Abigail.

"Trusting reliable information is what we ought to do to make up our minds about what we believe." Athens stated.

The angelic being gestured around them. "Look at all the images of these gods and goddesses before us. Those who crafted these figures believed that the gods would bless them for their worship. People often place things on a pedestal, even though they can never truly satisfy their needs for long. We have to be careful not to let our own desires and selfishness get in the way of God's plan."

Athens eyed the marble statues. One of the male figures held a trident, and one of the females held a spear in her hand and a shield in the other. Her eyebrows were furrowed together, and her lips pursed. She looked troubled.

"Do you ever ask yourself why you want something? Do you ever resist the temptation to have things? Do you understand?" asked the angelic being.

Abigail nodded her head. "Yeah, I totally get it. If we want the truth, sometimes we have to dig for it until we find it.

Abigail ran her finger across a stone statue and said, "It makes perfect sense. We often desire things without asking ourselves why, which can lead to poor decisions if we don't search for the truth first and ask the hard questions.

Sometimes, people are blinded from the real truth because they would rather hear something that makes them feel good."

"Staying focused on the mission ahead and searching for God's desires, instead of our own, will lead us to the truth. Now, will you please tell us who you are?" Athens asked.

A smile spread across her face. "I'm your guide. My name is Eliza, which means *God is my oath*. I've been sent here by Him to assist you."

"You mean God sent you?" Abigail inquired.

"Yes, The God in your dream. He's not just any ordinary god. He's the creator of the universe, the heavens, and the earth. Look around you; right before your eyes are the statues of many gods chiseled out of stone. Their powers were great but limited to their own dominions."

"You will soon discover that the God of the universe has many names, which will be revealed to you later.

He created all things and has raised you up for such a time as this. He has counted every hair on your head and has accounted for each one. He wants you to complete this quest by seeking the truth with all your heart, mind, and spirit. Remember to remain true in all you hear, all you think, all you see, and everything you say, and do. You must overcome all evil when confronted by it. Only then will your destiny be fulfilled."

Eliza continued. "Some of the gods, like Zeus, Apollo, and Poseidon were mighty in their day, but their powers were limited just like the goddess Athena's powers. She was the goddess of wisdom, and Aphrodite was the goddess of beauty and love. They sat on their thrones, having power and control over their kingdoms on the earth."

Without warning, a bolt of lightning struck down from heaven and smote the statue of Zeus, splitting its head and reducing it to rubble.

"What the heck?" Adrenaline pumped through Athens' veins as he reached for Abigail's hand, they began to run.

Eliza appeared before them like a twinkling light, holding out her hand as she signaled for them to stop.

Panting, Athens put his hands on his knees. "What was that?"

Abigail clutched her stomach. "I don't know, but it came out of nowhere."

Eliza put her hand over her mouth in awe and pointed to an incredible statue over their heads which had risen above the others.

Athens walked closer and looked upon the distinguished face of the image of a King. He appeared superior to the others, having piercing eyes, a round defined nose, heightened cheek bones and a strong jaw line. The title on the plaque read *The Unknown God.*

"The gods were seekers and lovers of themselves," she whispered. "They were always searching for their own glory and did not recognize the *Unknown God* as the One True God.

"They wanted dominion for themselves, so they rebelled against the One True God to their downfall. Their kingdoms crumbled, and all that remains of them are these ruins." Eliza ran her finger along a marble pillar. "It's best that we all walk the path which we were called to. You may not always receive the reward immediately, but all things will be fulfilled at the appointed time. Whether on Earth or in Heaven, it will be well worth the wait."

Athens smiled as he listened to her speak. He picked up a pebble from the ground and threw it.

"Everyone has a decision to make. To do good or to do evil." Eliza looked down at her hands and continued to speak, "Consider your choices... place truth in your right hand and deceit in your left hand. If you have trouble deciding which one to choose, put your hands together and pray." She paused for a moment.

"Did you know that you can ask God to help you make the right choice?" Eliza further said. "The key is in your own hands. Ask yourself the hard questions, then ask God to show you the truth and give you the strength to do what is right. <u>The power starts in your mind and moves to your heart and then your hands.</u>"

Athens folded his hands together. "Great point; I need to remember to do that from now on. It should work for any hard decision I have to make."

Then, his eyebrows rose with curiosity as he followed Eliza to a great stone near the cliff.

"This rock is your foundation. You must be standing on it in order to pass through the portal into each of the seven continents. This is where your faith steps in; without a solid foundation, you can't stand against the evil in the world, nor will you be able to move between continents. Only by speaking words of truth will you be granted the power to access the portal." She leaned in close to whisper in his ear, "Say these powerful words while standing on the rock when you are ready to move to the next continent, and you will arrive in that continent wearing their clothes and speaking their language. All of this is to help you blend in with the culture around you, so you don't appear to be an outsider."

"Are you ready?" Eliza asked.

He wiped his sweaty palms on his shirt and nodded.

Then Eliza told Athens the words: "Guide me in Your Truth and teach me Your ways, oh Lord, for You are my God, my Savior, my hope is in You all day long." Athens gazed at the ground. "Repeat those words three times to help you remember what to say because, without the exact words, there is no way to enter or exit any of the secret portals."

Athens began to speak the mighty words when he realized Abigail was no longer with him. "Where could she have gone?" he mumbled under his breath. "She has a habit of wandering off. I'm sorry, she sometimes gets easily distracted."

They looked toward the grassy area on the hill, by the brick watering well. From a distance, Athens could see Abigail behind a cluster of butterflies fluttering around the well. She had her arms outstretched and laughed when one landed on her nose.

Athens walked toward her and watched as she touched the flowers around the well. Some of them looked like miniature little monks kneeling and praying, and some looked like white doves sprouting from their stems. He continued watching as she climbed near the ledge.

She closed her eyes and leaned in to smell the flowers growing around the well, its sweet fragrance filled the air.

When she opened her eyes, a beautiful mammoth butterfly landed on her shoulder.

Athens picked up his pace and kept walking toward her, as she eyed the intricate detail of the butterfly. Then, she turned her head to gaze into the sparkling pool of water in the well. *Was she admiring herself?* She was staring at her reflection in the water as if bedazzled by her own beautiful, big brown eyes and long, silky, dark hair. Suddenly, she leaned in a little too far and fell into the well.

Athens gasped. He stretched out his arms to grab her, but he couldn't reach her. It was too late. He peered down into the deep hole as she spiraled downward out of control. She extended her arms and legs to slow herself down, but she continued to sink.

She opened her mouth to scream for help and words began forming in the water as they bubbled out of her mouth. Though no one could hear her.

Athens' heart constricted, making it difficult to breathe. He couldn't lose his best friend now. How could he save her? He looked around and noticed a bucket and a rope with a shiny buckle on it. There was no time to unwind it. When he picked it up, he felt a jolt of energy run through his body. He tossed it into the well, keeping a firm grip on the other end. *Could this be the Belt of Truth?* Strangely, he began to see the words *Truth, Hope, Faith,* and *Love* swirling around in the water, encircling Abigail. *Were those Abigail's words, or were they the wishes of other people?*

The magical belt wrapped itself perfectly around Abigail's waist. Slowly, Athens pulled her up to the surface and hoisted her out of the well.

Abigail choked on the water before spiting it out and gasped for air. Tears streamed down her cheeks as she stood there dripping wet. "I almost drowned," she sobbed. "I panicked until I saw the long, silver belt that appeared in front of me. I was so vain to gape at myself the way that I did. I was admiring my reflection in the water, and then I guess I leaned in a little too far and fell in. I'm so sorry. I could've jeopardized the mission. Will you please forgive me?"

Athens wrapped his arm around her. "It's alright, we all struggle in our own areas. I'm just glad you're okay; this could have ended very badly if the belt hadn't appeared."

Eliza drew closer and said, "You have to be more careful, Abigail. Think about what you're doing and why you're doing it; It's good to be mindful of your actions. Never compare yourself to others. Everyone is unique and wonderfully made. Now, let's go over to the rock and finish preparing for departure."

They followed Eliza back to where the rock was, then she motioned in the air and the rock magically appeared. "When you stand on the rock, your standing on a firm foundation that cannot be shaken."

Athens nodded his head as he prepared his stance and said, "God is kind of like this rock; He's rock solid, something that you can put your weight on. He allows you to walk through life's challenges, but He always walks through them with you, even though it may not feel like it."

Then, Eliza pressed her hands together and straightened her stance. "Let's go over the words again to make sure you're ready."

"Sounds good." Athens added as he moved in closer.

Eliza recited the words for them: "Guide me in Your truth and teach me Your ways, oh Lord, for You are my God, my Savior, my hope is in You all day long." Then she pointed to Athens and asked him to repeat it.

Athens began to speak the words, and Abigail mouthed the words just in case he happened to forget any.

Then Eliza told them, "After you speak the words, spin around and you'll teleport to the next continent. It all happens in the blink of an eye." Eliza took a step back and said, "There's a rock in each of the places you'll be venturing to; they'll usually be near a landmark of some sort. You must return to the rock to pass on to the next region."

Athens pulled out the onyx globe that his parents had given him. "We can use my globe to trace our steps."

"Your globe is quite remarkable," Eliza said.

"I received it as an early birthday gift," Athens exclaimed. "We can look at the globe to view all the continents. It will show us where we've been and where we need to go. It also has the power to show us glimpses of the prize ahead, which will keep us motivated to press on."

Eliza reached out and touched the globe, putting her finger on Egypt. "When you get there, you'll need to search for the Breastplate of Righteousness in the Valley of the Kings. Don't forget that you only have 24 hours to find each armor piece, covering all seven continents in just seven days. You must understand the meaning of each armor piece once you find them; It's of great importance for you to know how and when to use them. As you collect and put on each piece of armor, you will grow in faith and power."

Athens held the globe close to his chest and Abigail put her hands over her heart as she stared into the globe.

"Don't forget to guard your mind, heart, and soul. And guard the truth with your life." Eliza stated.

Athens and Abigail took a step of faith and stood firmly on the rock. Then, Athens spoke the powerful words, and they both spun around, as a mighty gust of wind blew in and swept them away.

CHAPTER 2

Who is the Righteous One?

BREASTPLATE OF RIGHTEOUSNESS

The Valley of the Kings, Egypt

"Whoa, that was awesome! It felt like we just traveled through a time warp at the speed of light." Athens said. "It all happens so fast. The tingling sensation was incredible. I felt as light as a feather." Fluttered Abigail.

I'm definitely looking forward to doing that again.

"Night began to fall as they entered Egypt. Athens and Abigail were excited, yet a little disoriented from the transport. They were standing on the rock's edge near the Nile River, dressed in charming Egyptian clothing.

A moment later, Eliza showed up like a beaming light to warn them of the dangers in Egypt. "After the sun goes down, The Valley of the Kings is where robbers hide and where strange creatures go lurking about, seeking prey to devour."

Athens didn't seem to be worried about the dangers ahead. But shouldn't he be? He appeared more curious about the things which lay ahead. He wondered which great kings of antiquity might be buried there. No matter what, he was ready to conquer whatever crossed his path. *"What do you think the kings were thinking when they built such elaborate tombs for themselves?"* he whispered.

He imagined them eating and drinking and living merry lives.

Athens bent down and picked up a half-broken piece of a stone tablet from the ground, bearing the mark of a sphinx then looked at Eliza.

"What do you know about the kings of old?" he asked.

She straightened her stance and met his gaze. "Well," she said confidently. "Around 500 BC, King Tut, King Ramses, and many other Pharaohs lived very luxurious lives with the hope of someday escaping the clutches of death. They built secret ceremonial chambers and had elaborate tombs to preserve their royal dead bodies that were hidden away. Vessels filled with jewels, food and drinks were kept for their pleasure in the afterlife. This was their grand scheme."

Eliza further stated. "What they didn't realize, is that no amount of silver, gold, or gods could bring them back to their physical life on Earth to continue living out their lives. Over the centuries, treasure hunters and tomb raiders have stolen almost everything. Thieves sold, traded, or kept the treasures for themselves. Most everything else was destroyed or placed in museums. It's believed that the kings and pharaohs of old never recognized the King of kings, the only One who could have truly given them the gift of eternal Life. This King loves all people, rich and poor, young, and old alike. This King gave His own life as a ransom to save millions of other lives, including yours and mine; Only a righteous King would do such a thing for His people. The greatest news is that this King rose from the dead, and those who trust in Him are also raised to a new life!"

Unfolding her arms, Abigail interrupted with a question. "You mean *everyone* lives forever?"

"Yes!" Eliza said. Her eyes were crystal clear. "That's exactly what I mean. The One True King wants to save every lost soul and help every single person come to know and accept the truth. He wants you to be filled with love, peace, and forgiveness. It can't be bought, sold, or taken away from you, no matter what others say or do."

Abigail's eyes popped open wide as she smiled. "Imagine if everyone you met was kind and thoughtful. How wonderful that would be!"

"Yeah, that would be a miracle." Athens smiled as he looked up into the heavens and noticed a spectacular starlight in the night sky. "I can see Leo the lion's constellation."

Abigail pointed to the Big Dipper and the Little Dipper, too.

"Let's keep going. We don't have much time." Eliza directed them to the north and showed them the Star of Bethlehem and told them it hadn't been seen for over two thousand years; It shone bright against the black sky. It was yet another heavenly sign of the One True King.

A grand and fierce lion with a beautiful golden mane appeared on the horizon. He raised his head in the air and could smell the human scent from afar as he caught a glimpse of them, sizing them up for a possible meal. Athens looked off into the distance to the top of the hill; he could make out the silhouettes of a herd of lions sitting behind their king on the rocks. These majestic animals were a reminder of who was in charge of the animal kingdom.

Athens shuddered. He certainly didn't want to be their next meal. He looked ahead and saw the crossroads leading down separate paths. Thinking about which way to go, something blew across the ground that looked a lot like tumbleweed as it stopped right in front of his feet. At a closer look, it appeared to be a ball of little flowers, but as a whole it looked like a humungous rose. Athens knelt down to pick it up and then smelled it. What was it? It appeared to be some sort of a plant.

"This is a Resurrection plant, also known as the Rose of Jericho," Eliza said. "It can survive for years without water. It tumbles around on the ground in search of water until it finds some, then it stops to drink it up and blossoms wherever it happens to be."

"So, it never needs to be planted in the ground?" asked Abigail.

"Nope. It's a marvelous plant really," Eliza replied.

Athens shifted the plant in his hands, examining it closer and then set it back down on the ground. Out of the corner of his eye, Athens noticed a sign with many arrows pointing in different directions. The first arrow read *Lincoln the Lion's Den,* and pointed to a long, narrow path facing the hillside. Another sign pointed down a path that was broad and crooked; it read *Lucifer the Dragon's Lair,* and a big *X* was painted over it. The third sign pointed down a short, bumpy path that read *Jaxon the Jaguar's Cove.*

"One path will lead you in the right direction while the other paths will lead you astray," Eliza said pointing to the signs.

Athens kicked the dirt. None of the options seemed like a good idea, but if he had to choose one, he'd choose the narrow path toward the lion's den. No way would he choose the broad way leading to Lucifer's lair.

"It's time to choose," Eliza urged.

Just then, a handsome young man with dark thick hair and dimples appeared on the same path as them. He saw the Resurrection plant, picked it up, and then put it in his bag. "This will be quite useful." He turned toward Athens. "This plant is said to bring blessings and prosperity to anyone who possesses it. I bet I can make a fortune selling these in the marketplace. I just need to learn how to grow them first."

"Come on, we've got to go," Athens called out, as he fixed Abigail with a stare.

"Where are you going?" asked the young man.

"We're on a grand mission searching for sacred armor. Right now, we're looking for the breastplate, but our final destination is in Israel. By the way, I'm Athens, and who are you?" Athens reached out to shake his hand.

"Addison's my name. I'm on my way to Israel too. Do you mind if I tag along?"

Athens wiped his hand over his face. It didn't seem right to tell him no, but hopefully he wasn't another roadblock, like the well. "Okay, you can join us if you're up for an adventure; this trip is not for the fainthearted. But you'll have to leave the plant here. Where we're going, you won't need to worry about money."

Addison gave him a curious look and laughed like he thought he was joking, then realized no one else was laughing so he put the plant back on the ground and left it there.

The three of them decided to head toward the lion's den, which led past a golden field of wheat and lavender just before reaching the Valley of the Kings. Without warning, a fierce lion rustled in the field in front of them. His tawny coat and golden mane were visible through the wheat field, his pride snuck up behind them for an ambush.

The lion let out a tremendous roar as they stood in the field, gazing hungrily at Athens and his friends.

Athens, without thinking, bravely held up his hand and shouted, "Stop!"

The other lions slowly moved in and formed a circle around them. They were surrounded.

Athens trembled but stood bravely against them. If he couldn't get the lions to listen, they'd all be mincemeat. "I said stop in the name of the One True King!"

Lincoln the lion was about to leap into the air to pounce on Athens, when an angel of the Lord appeared and stopped him.

Then Lincoln stopped, and bowed before Athens. "Forgive me master Athens, I didn't recognize you."

Stunned that the lion could speak. Athens hesitated before answering. "Not a problem, I'm just glad you're not going to eat us." Athens arched his back and stood tall.

Lincoln the lion was captivated by the power of God's Spirit who protected them. The lion was also told to provide Athens and his friends with protection against the wild things of the night. Lincoln no longer desired to eat them. Instead, he led them by a secret way through a great cave to the mouth of the lion's den, where they gazed upon a giant monument carved into the stone. The entire monument was in the shape of a lion.

The entrance of the den was shaped like a giant lion's head. Its mouth had sharp jagged teeth to keep people away. Dense vines kept it well hidden. Just above them, Athens uncovered an inscription that read: *Only a true righteous one with a pure heart should dare enter this dwelling, lest you should die.*

Addison folded his arms across his chest. "No way am I going in there."

"You don't have to. I'll go in by myself." Athens stepped forward.

"I'm coming with you." Abigail lifted her chin.

"No. You wait here," Athens insisted.

She shook her head. "Nope. We both had the dream. We're doing this together."

Athens cracked a smile and took out his onyx globe as they walked toward the giant stone head of the lion. They proceeded inside when a ray of light beamed from the onyx globe. The light magically caused an opening to appear guiding them into an inner chamber filled with magnificent armor, stretching across the entire room.

Athens scratched the back of his head. How did this happen and how was he supposed to choose the right one? He turned to the right, then turned to the left and knelt down on one knee. Which breastplate would represent his King?

He closed his eyes, trying to imagine which ones were used in battle and which one may have been worn by the High Priests of the Royal Priesthood. What was it like living back in those days? Who would have worn the Breastplate of Righteousness? Still considering his options, he placed his hands together and prayed, seeking wisdom from God.

He emptied his mind of any thoughts he had about the breastplate and waited for the Lord to reveal which one he should choose. When nothing immediately happened, he got up, and tried his best not to get impatient.

He moved slowly along the wall, touching row after row of armor. Some were made of various metals, some had relics indicating royalty, and others had emblems of swords and crosses on them. "Do you see anything that could be the right one, Abigail?"

She didn't answer.

Athens turned in a circle, with his eyes peeled.

She was nowhere in sight.

Ugh. Where did she go? Before he could think about it for too long, a particular breastplate caught his eye. It had characteristics unique to the others. It was adorned with twelve exquisite gems and each had a brilliant glowing hue. The armor was made of fine purple, blue, and scarlet linen.

The shoulder straps were braided chains of gold, with a sizable black onyx stone set in gold on the top of each shoulder. Above each of the twelve stones were engraved the names of the twelve tribes of Israel.

This had to be it. Without another thought, Athens reached out and took it off the armor stand. It shimmered as he pulled it over his head to dress himself with it. It was a perfect fit. It was not at all what he had expected; he thought it would be solid metal like something a soldier would wear into battle, but it wasn't. It was much better. An explosion of confidence came over him. His heart was filled with gladness as he stood dressed in righteousness.

Now, he had to find Abigail. Athens walked down the hall, as he called out, "Abigail? Where are you? I found it! I found the breastplate!"

His words were met with silence.

After a few minutes, he came across an opening that led him out into a valley where many dry bones were scattered on the ground. In the middle of the bones, an ancient book laid in the rubble, covered in dirt.

Athens maneuvered through the bones, being careful not to step on them as he grabbed the book. What is this? He was about to dust it off when snarling and snapping noises echoed behind him. The blood rushed out of his face. His heart raced as he turned to face the growling noise.

A few feet away, two black jaguars with razor-sharp teeth and claws stared at him. One raced toward him, then lunged into the air, and pounced on him, pinning him to the ground. Saliva dripped from the creature's mouth and landed on Athens' cheek.

Its eyes narrowed into thin slits. Athens' heart was thumping so loud he could hear it, but there was something behind the animal's eyes. Intelligence? Maybe these jaguars were keepers of the armor. It would be their job to stop anyone from taking it out of the valley. Perhaps this was Jaxon the jaguar.

Whoever the creature was, Athens had to get away. Using all his strength, he tried to push the creature off of him, but the jaguar was too strong. Two stones burst off the vest from the force of the hit and landed next to Athens. *"Thank you, God."* He stretched out his arm as far as he could, straining for the two precious stones.

The jaguar pulled back one of its front legs, then stamped its foot on Athens' arm, squeezing its claws into his skin.

Athens screamed out in pain. Jaxon's friend leaned over Athens' face and let out a menacing cackle. "Any last words before we devour you?"

***

While Athens had been examining the armor, Abigail had discovered a side-passage leading down into another hall. She was fascinated by the great tombs deep within the mountain. She ran her hand along the ancient engravings on the wall. Abigail longed to see what Cleopatra's tomb looked like, so she began searching for it but came across an old book covered in dust and cobwebs sitting beside a sarcophagus. Not thinking about the breastplate, she knelt down and started reading the inscription on it. Her voice echoed through the halls as she translated out loud, causing a stirring from the sarcophagi where the mummies slumbered. As she read a list of names, loud groans filled the air. The lids on the sarcophagus creaked open, and withered faces wrapped in cloth peered out. She had no idea the book would summon the mummies from their tombs. Her mouth dropped open and she screamed. Her voice was thick with fear. "Athens!"

***

Athens trembled and was stunned at the thought of another talking animal. "Wait! Please, don't eat me; God sent me here to claim the armor. I must take it to King Elohim. It's one of six pieces I've been searching for, and I must have it."

The jaguar smirked. "Oh sure, God sent *you*. Where is this God of yours?"

He ran his tongue along his teeth. "How old are you anyway?"

"I'm fourteen."

A wicked smile spread across the other jaguar's face. "You'll never get out of here alive."

Jaxon was still sitting on Athens' chest. "Why should I believe you?" Athens shifted slightly and reached for the stones again, this time wrapping his hand around them. The stones illuminated brightly through his fist.

"Do not harm him." A booming voice echoed from above. *"Let him go."*

Jaxon lifted his paw but stayed put. A third and unusual jaguar appeared out of nowhere and slunk over to whisper in Jaxon's ear. "No, don't let him go. We can eat him for a midnight snack."

Jaxon snarled. "Be silent."

Jaxon's friend pounced in between them and sank his teeth into the back of the third, unusual jaguar's neck. The unusual jaguar extended his claws and roared as Jaxon's friend slung him into a great stone.

Athens sat up slowly. His chest rose and fell. Thank God, the jaguars no longer wanted to eat him. His gaze then traveled to the ancient book. He leaned over and picked it up, then brushed off the rubble, and opened it. The book's pages whimsically flipped back and forth until he put his hand in the middle of it to stop the flow; the words magically floated off the pages and came alive. It read, *"He who has ears let him hear."*

"Oh son of man, hear my words," the book proceeded. Just then, a strong gust of wind blew as Athens continued reading. *"Prophesy to these bones and say to them, O' you dry bones, hear the word of the Lord! Behold, I will cause breath and spirit to enter you, and you shall live: I will bring forth muscles and flesh upon you and cover you with skin, and you shall return to your own land in Israel and live so you can know that I am the living God, a sovereign ruler who calls for Truth and Righteousness."* Athens paused to take a deep breath.

A loud thundering noise shook the earth's surface, and the bones that were scattered all over the ground began to rattle. The wind blew mightily, and the voice of God spoke over them. Skeletons formed together and stood on their feet. Muscles & tendons formed over their bones, new skin formed over their muscles. Eyes miraculously formed inside their sockets. The bones had become a host of men.

Thoughts permeated through Athens' mind as he stood in awe of what had just unfolded before him and the power of the book.

"Athens!" Abigail's scream rang throughout the cave.

He shut the book and tucked it under his arm as he raced back toward the hallway, toward her voice. "I'm coming. Don't move." He turned a corner and collided with a mummy.

Athens stumbled backward. This mummy wasn't in a crypt, but stood upright and its bandages loosened from the force of their collision. A piece of cloth got caught on the corner of Athens' breastplate and wouldn't come loose. The mummy was acting frantic; It was moving its limbs wildly until it came completely unraveled.

As the last few pieces unraveled around its head, long brown strands of hair fell loose around its shoulders. *Abigail?*

Athens almost laughed. He broke the space between them and wrapped his arms around her. "What happened to you?"

"I accidentally woke the mummies. There are more of them and they're coming after us." Abigail stated.

"Seriously?" Athens exclaimed.

"Uh-huh. No time to explain. Let's go." Abigail waved at him. "Follow me. I think I know the way out." She ran in a new direction, down a dark, narrow tunnel.

Heavy footsteps followed behind them and groans crept from every direction.

At the end of the tunnel, Athens skidded to a stop. The path had them back to the Valley of Dry Bones. The dry bones, now living men, stood at attention as if waiting for Athens to hurdle past them.

A second later the men saw the mummies, they rushed forward, moving swiftly past Athens and Abigail to charge the mummies and defend God's anointed. It was clear that the spirit of God rose-up inside of the men after they saw Athens wearing the Breastplate of Righteousness.

Athens and Abigail escaped the valley during the brawl and ran to the transportation stone near the Nile River. Where was Addison? Where was Eliza?

Athens and Abigail couldn't risk waiting any longer. They needed to complete their quest with or without Addison. Hopefully, Eliza would show up when she was needed.

Athens and Abigail stepped onto the rock and spoke the words while spinning, "Guide me in Your truth and teach me Your ways, oh Lord, for You are my God, my Savior, my hope is in You all day long."

In the blink of an eye, a gust of wind whirled around them, and swooped them up into midair as they disappeared.

CHAPTER 3

A Leap of Faith

GOSPEL SHOES OF PEACE

Canberra, Australia

Stepping off the rock into the heat of Australia's outback, Athens and Abigail became curious when they noticed a strange wind blowing around from the far south. Dark clouds blanketed the sky as a gigantic cloud of dust began swirling about, and slowly grew into a tornado; two red eyes mysteriously formed out of the center of it. *Could this giant tornado be a dust devil?*

Abigail's eyes widened. "What in the world is that?" she asked.

The moment she spoke, the dust devil began spiraling in their direction.

"It looks like it's headed our way. Let's get out of here!" said Athens.

They swiftly zigzagged across the loose ground, kicking up the dirt beneath their feet, leaving a cloud of dust behind them.

The monstrous dust devil weaved back and forth toward them as if it had a mind of its own. Athens felt the wind blowing all around as they ran. He pushed Abigail to move faster. The winds continued growing stronger and debris gathered in the air and got sucked up into the dust devil. But it didn't slow it down, it continued gaining speed.

Abigail's breathing became more difficult with each passing step.

Seconds later, heavier winds blew in from the west, creating another massive whirlwind.

"If we don't run faster, we'll get sucked up in it," Athens shouted over the roaring wind.

Suddenly, lightning shot down from the sky, creating brilliant sparks and flashes of light with piercing gold embers that caused some tumbleweed on the ground to catch fire. The tumbleweeds blew directly into the center of the whirlwind, setting it ablaze.

Athens glanced at Abigail.

Her eyes widened further, and her bottom lip trembled. "We're in big trouble." She said.

Out of nowhere, a large troop of kangaroos came scurrying by to escape the tornado's flames. One of the babies jumped out of his mother's pouch.

"Oh no," yelled Athens. "Come on, Abigail, let's go get him." Without waiting for her response, he dashed after the little kangaroo to return him to his mother, but the little kangaroo was too fast. Finally exhausted from running, and out of harm's way, Athens shouted, "Hey, little joey, stop!"

As the kangaroo heard Athens' voice, he stopped in his tracks. Standing right in front of a small village, the kangaroo turned around and asked, "How did you know my name?"

Athens also stopped in his tracks. *Did that baby kangaroo just speak?* When the animal repeated the question, Athens shook his head and answered. "Well, I have a friend named Joey, and he's the fastest runner I know. You reminded me of him," Athens just smiled. He turned to Abigail. "Doesn't he remind you of Joey? Wait, what am I saying?" He smacked his forehead.

She didn't respond.

Athens scanned the area, but Abigail wasn't around. However, he did catch sight of a village nearby and decided to begin making his way over there with the baby kangaroo.

As they were walking, Athens asked, "So what were you doing anyway?" The kangaroo responded, "I was scared and thought the tornado was going to get me, so I ran away."

"Would you mind helping me find my friend?" Athens asked, feeling a little safer now that they were inside the village.

"Sure," said the kangaroo.

Athens continued, "I'm not sure which way she went, but I need to find her. We're on a global quest... a grand mission, traveling around the world in search of six armor pieces. Right now, I'm searching for the Gospel Shoes of Peace."

Some of the villagers were curious about Athens and Little Joey, so they peeked out of their clay homes, that resembled the shapes of beehives, to see what was going on.

"Either of these swirling storms could kill us all and destroy the village. We have to get out of here," said Little Joey.

"I've never seen anything like them," Athens said. "Let me say a quick prayer to my God."

"Who's your God?" asked Little Joey.

Athens replied, "He's the God of the universe who created the heavens and the earth. He guides and protects me and is here to help whenever I call on His name. You can call on Him too and He'll hear you. Actually, anyone can call on Him. He loves and cares about us and created us to have a true relationship with Him.

Athens further stated, "God gave me a dream, and now I'm living it out. He has gone to prepare a place in His kingdom for me to possess after I complete His quest. In this kingdom, there are splendid mansions made with precious stone and the streets there are even made of gold."

Little Joey leaped into the air, and so did Athens.

Athens continued to share what he knew about God, forgetting about the dust devil. "His kingdom has divine riches and treasures beyond your wildest dreams. The things of this world are temporary, but the things we inherit from the Kingdom of God will last forever. He gives us the ability to accomplish great things when we trust in Him." Athens glanced around.

"You see, it's here in the desert that the Gospel Shoes of Peace must be found before I can travel to the next continent. I must deliver all the armor pieces to King Elohim on the seventh and final day to receive my inheritance."

Athens showed him the belt and breastplate. Little Joey was mesmerized at the sight of them and wanted to touch them but was afraid to ask.

As Athens and Joey were speaking, Athens noticed a plume of smoke in the distance. He saw that it was rising from the ruins of an ancient tower, which was just burned by the dust devil.

An older woman from the village, with sun-soaked skin and silver hair, approached Athens and Joey, and said, "It's believed that people of every tribe and nation spoke one language thousands of years ago; they tried building this tower to reach into the heavens and challenge God. This made God angry, so He did not allow them to accomplish this thing. He confused their languages so the people could no longer understand each other or cooperate to continue building the tower. The tower was eventually deserted, and the people moved away to settle in other regions around the world."

The massive, burning tornado suddenly appeared at the border of the little village. They had waited too long to escape. A voice came from the fierce, fiery tornado and spoke directly to Athens.

"Do not be afraid. It is I, the Lord, your God, who is with you and will not harm you. Now step into the Holy flames and receive the Gospel Shoes of Peace."

Athens took a deep breath. God had been faithful so far; he had prevented the lion from eating him and the jaguars from attacking him. Athens had to trust that God would do it again.

Swallowing hard, Athens mustered up his courage and stepped into the fire before he could change his mind. The flames covered him from head to toe as he stood in the presence of God. Completely saturated by God's Holy Spirit, Athens was baptized in flames. Not one hair on his head was singed, nor did his clothing burn or reek of smoke.

Instantly, the Gospel Shoes of Peace were firmly fitted on his feet.

With his eyes closed, Athens began praising God. Suddenly, his speech magically became words that were unknown to him, and he spoke in an ancient language which he had never heard before.

When Athens opened his eyes, the village people stared at him as if they understood what he had said. It must have been in their native tongue.

Athens looked down at his feet in amazement. A tingling sensation ran down his spine. "Hallelujah," he shouted. "I can't believe I'm wearing the Gospel Shoes of Peace. Praise God!"

As Athens spoke, the dangerous dirt devil spun up not far behind them. Debris was sailing through the air. The Fiery Tornado which Athens had just been inside grew to great enormity, seven times the size of the dust devil. The Great Fiery Tornado swept over the dust devil and consumed it with eternal fire. Nothing remained but smoke, soot and ashes.

Little Joey's jaw dropped wide open. "Praise God." Joey leaped for joy. "Now, we can tell others what we have seen with our own eyes!"

Then, the Fiery Tornado turned away from the people and vanished into thin air.

"God's mighty power truly exists!" one of the villagers shouted. "We are forever honored and will always remember this day. Even though I couldn't see God, I felt His presence in the wind."

Little Joey and the villagers had witnessed their very first miracle. They thought the fire was going to kill them, but instead, it saved them.

"Now that I have received the Gospel Shoes of Peace, I have to get going and share the good news. I'm on my way to meet King Elohim," Athens declared.

Little Joey jumped up and down. "Who's King Elohim?"

"King Elohim was the King in my dream. He's called me to complete this quest, and if I can accomplish it, I'll become an heir to His kingdom. I have learned the meaning of His name—One True King. He gives the gift of Eternal Life to anyone who chooses to believe in Him."

"I believe, I believe!" Little Joey exclaimed. "Even though I can't see Him I can feel His presence just like the wind."

Then Athens said, "God has given me a new spirit and a new heart, and it looks like He has done the same for you. Now, let's go find Abigail and your mom. I don't know which way Abigail went, so let's ask God to guide us." Athens bowed his head and prayed, "Lord of lords, King of kings, creator of all things, please help us find Abigail and Little Joey's mom. Most of all, thank you for protecting us from harm and for giving me the Gospel Shoes of Peace."

Athens and Joey continued praising God as they walked past the border of the village. They could see the troop of kangaroos a little beyond where the dust devil had passed through and came to the edge of the little settlement. As they walked closer, Athens wondered where Abigail might be; but just then, he saw her head pop up from behind the kangaroos. Relief flooded through him. "I'm glad you're all right Abigail! What happened to you?"

Abigail replied, "I got a little anxious because of the dirt devil, and then somehow I got lost in the herd of kangaroos as I was following behind you, and then you disappeared. Where did you go?" Right when Athens was about to tell her, Little Joey's mom hopped over and embraced him. She kissed little Joey's head, then glanced at Athens and said, "Thank you for returning my son! I was looking everywhere for him. How can I ever repay you?"

Athens replied, "No worries, ma'am. Although I am a little hungry; do you know where we could find any food?"

Suddenly out of the clouds, manna came pouring down from heaven like an unexpected rainfall. Everyone, including the villagers, looked up in awe. The villagers ran back to their bee hive homes to grab their hand-woven baskets. Then they held the baskets over their heads and tried to catch the manna. The villagers made a game out of catching the manna, so whenever some landed in their baskets, they would shout and cheer.

Athens smiled. "Wow, this is amazing!"

"I've never seen anything like it." Abigail nodded, fully looking at him for the first time since the storm; Her gaze rested on his feet. "You found the Gospel Shoes of Peace!"

"Yeah, I had to walk inside the flames. When I did, the shoes appeared on my feet." He replied.

Then Abigail shouted with excitement. "Woohoo! Hallelujah! Now, we can go to Rio de Janeiro, Brazil, to find the Shield of Faith."

Athens turned to Little Joey. "I'm sorry buddy, we have to go now. We're running out of time. Abigail and I hope to see you again someday."

***

Athens and Abigail were on their way back to the rock when Athens started thinking about the Great Barrier Reef. He was hopelessly curious. He couldn't help but wonder what it would be like to swim in the great ocean for even just a moment. It was his lifelong dream. The sea's depths, the glistening blue waves, the cool ocean breeze, and the warm, soft sand running through his toes were all he could think about.

"Hey Abigail, let's go for a swim! We may never have the chance to see the great barrier reef again, so let's take advantage of the opportunity!"

"Ha ha, I think I'll sit this one out, I'm not really in the mood to swim right now."

***

Abigail sat on a rock as Athens walked down to the beach. He took off his armor pieces and placed them inside of his backpack, then dove into the deep blue ocean.

Laughing, Abigail shook her head. She watched his head bob in and out of the water for a few minutes as the waves brushed over his head. After a while she became restless and began wiggling her feet into the warm sand while Athens enjoyed himself in the ocean, then she decided to go exploring instead of just sitting there.

She got up and strolled across the sandy beach, soaking in the sights. Up ahead, a flock of birds wrestled along the ocean bank. As she drew near, the birds squeaked and squawked. She giggled, then went gliding right through the middle of them. Hundreds of birds were everywhere. Some flew high, some flew low and some barely moved at all.

All of a sudden, Abigail felt something hot touch her toe. "Ouch!" She reached down and sifted through the sand to see what it was and picked up a shiny silver cross necklace with an inscription that read *"God loves you."* She clutched the cross to her chest. *What a special treasure.* She placed it around her neck and continued walking, this time farther inland, until she came to a garden sanctuary a little way off from the beach. There was a sign at the entrance that read, *"Do not taste the fruit of this garden."*

That's odd. Why would the fruit be forbidden? Curiosity itched at Abigail's mind as she walked into the garden. Near the entrance, there were many diverse fruit trees that had a delicious fragrance that filled the air. Beyond these trees, a little farther she found a beautiful painted forest of eucalyptus trees. It appeared as though an artist had splattered brightly colored paint all over the trunks of these trees. *How magnificent!* She drew closer to the painted eucalyptus trees, so she could run her fingers along them to feel the texture of them. The unique scent of the blossoms floated into her nose.

Abigail peered up into the trees and couldn't resist picking an incredibly plump and juicy apple, even though the sign said not to.

As she opened her mouth to take a bite, something tugged on the back of her hair.

She turned around and noticed a sloth sitting on a low branch in the tree she was standing under. The creature stared at her as if it was admiring her, then dropped onto her head, holding on tight.

Abigail gasped. "Whoa! What are you doing?"

"Sorry, I didn't mean to scare you." The sloth slid down into her arms. "I should've introduced myself first. I'm Savannah."

Abigail rubbed her head; the sloth must have landed harder than she'd realized. No way was this animal talking to her. It wasn't possible. Then again, most of their journey seemed impossible. Maybe the sloth could talk, after all. *She paused.* "Um, I'm Abigail."

"What a pretty name." Savannah shifted in her arms and the name tag attached to her collar jingled.

Abigail replied, "Oh, you must belong to someone. How did you get here? I wish I could take you with me; you're so cute."

Savannah smiled and handed Abigail another large apple. "A friend of the forest put me here to keep me safe from poachers."

"Thank you for the apple. Will you be all right if I go? I need to get back to my friend," Abigail said.

The sloth gave a slow nod and climbed up to her branch.

Footsteps were approaching. "Glad I found you," Athens said.

Abigail jumped and her hand flew to her chest. "You scared me."

"Sorry," Athens chuckled. "I had the most incredible swim with a humpback whale. It was the most graceful, and yet gigantic creature I've ever seen." He looked down at her hands and saw the two pieces of delicious fruit. "Where did you get the apples?"

"It came from one of these trees," Abigail replied.

Athens' eyebrows furrowed together. "Didn't you see the sign at the entrance?"

"Yes, but I think it'll be okay. Something so luscious can't possibly be bad for you."

Athens shrugged. "Can I have one?"

"Of course." She handed him an apple and took a big bite of her own. Then Athens took a bite of his. Their legs became wobbly, their vision soon blurred, and the world around them went black as they slumped down to the ground.

***

Back in the outback, Eliza showed up like a sparkling light and waited at the edge of the desert near the rock. She noticed an inspiring, male peacock spider dancing on top of the rock. He was brilliantly colored and was just about the size of a grain of rice. He wasn't about to move off the rock until he captured the attention of one of the lovely female spiders. After a while, one of the females glanced his way and advanced toward him. All it took was one look for her to fall in love. The two spiders mingled and danced then spun their way off the rocks edge.

By now, Eliza knew something was amiss, so she went searching for Athens and Abigail. She found them lying asleep just outside of the garden forest and knew something wasn't right. They must have fallen under a spell. Eliza swiftly gathered some water from the ocean nearby and tossed it on the two of them. They immediately opened their eyes and gasped for air. Now it was near dawn the next day.

"Hurry up, there isn't much time! You won't get another chance to meet the King," Eliza exclaimed as she moved them to their feet. "I see you didn't obey the sign that warned you about eating the fruit. I hope it's not too late."

"Oh! About that, I didn't have my armor on. I think if I would've been wearing it, I could've resisted eating the apple," Athens said as he held up the backpack that still contained the armor pieces.

"Yes, you would have... With your armor, you could have helped Abigail resist also. But it doesn't matter now; what is done is done. Let's press on." Eliza hurried them both to the rock and waited while Athens spoke the powerful words. The pair quickly spun around and disappeared in a heartbeat.

CHAPTER 4

Conquering Your Fears

SHIELD OF FAITH

Rio de Janeiro, Brazil

Arriving in South America, Athens and Abigail were wearing fun summer clothing. Their view of the lush green terrain was astonishing. They could see the sky-scraping mountains peaking off into the distance. Abigail became thrilled at the thought of finding their next piece of armor in Rio de Janeiro.

Eliza twirled in like a sparkling gem. "Did I mention that you'll see one of the seven wonders of the world? It will be life-changing for both of you. The whole world marvels at the magnificent sight of *Christ The Redeemer* Monument. It's there that you must find the Shield of Faith." Eliza pointed her finger into the air. "But first, I have a surprise for you."

"Really? What is it?" Athens and Abigail both said at the same time.

"Look behind you." She said.

Addison was standing behind them wearing a charming smile, he raised his hands in the air. "It'll be an amazing sight to see."

"Yes, it will!" Abigail said as she hugged his neck.

"It's nice to see you again, my friend," Athens admitted.

"It'll be quite exhilarating to actually climb to the top!" Abigail turned toward the mountain as she spoke.

"Yes, I can't wait," Addison confirmed with another smile as he stretched his hands behind his head and twisted from side to side while checking out the scenery.

Athens didn't respond. Climbing to the top was not his idea of a good time.

Looking around, they spotted an amusement park not far away. Abigail pointed at a billboard that read, *The Greatest Show on Earth!* Behind the sign, carnival rides and games were scattered across a huge field. Addison picked up a blue flyer off the ground and read it. "There's a parade with fun-filled festivities and food. They even have an epic helicopter ride and hot air balloons."

"I hope they have blueberry cotton candy. That's my favorite," Abigail said with delight.

"Have you ever been in a hot air balloon before?" Addison asked.

"Nope, and I don't ever plan on it," Athens responded. "I've never cared for heights." He looked up at the Ferris wheel. No way would he ever ride one.

"I've been on plenty of them, and they're a lot of fun. You can see everything from miles away when you're sitting up so high. It's like being on top of the world!" Abigail exclaimed as she twirled her hair.

Eliza shook her angelical head. "I'm sorry, but there's no time to waste. Your nap in the forest has cost you time that you now have to make up. I'm glad everyone is in great shape for the hike because it will definitely be tiring. The mountain range is very high and the air is thin."

In Truth, Athens had a fear of heights, but deep down inside, he knew that facing his fear was the only way to overcome it.

Abigail gave Athens a sympathetic look and asked Eliza, "Is there anything we can do to help Athens overcome his fear of heights?"

"There are many ways to overcome fear. One way is not to think about what you are doing, focus on something else, and press forward. Imagine something you love to do and envision yourself doing it. Singing also is a good way to distract yourself from fear. It's said that music is the bridge between heaven and earth," Eliza said while Abigail moved her hand back and forth as if stroking a violin.

"You could think of someone who would cheer you on, and then pretend like you're doing it for them," Abigail added as she batted her eyes.

"Another way is to imagine that you're rescuing someone from danger and their life depends on it," Addison suggested.

"Better yet, take long, deep breaths while focusing on your nose and mouth. Breathe in through your nose and exhale out of your mouth," Abigail sighed.

Eliza continued, "Believe in yourself. Tell yourself that you can do it. Say it out loud." She placed her hands around her mouth to direct the sound. Most importantly, pray and talk to God. Ask Him to strengthen you, giving you more faith and courage. He knows you can't do it alone."

"That's something my mom would say," Athens sighed.

Eliza looked into Athens eyes. "Never give doubt, worries, or fear the chance to creep into your mind and infect your thoughts; they will debilitate you if you give them too much power. Be strong, be brave, be courageous!"

Athens gave a shaky smile. "Thanks, everybody; I've got the idea. Now, I need to put the armor of God back on. Climbing to the top of the monument will strengthen my mind, my body, and my spirit too. It isn't going to be easy, but I believe with His help, I can do anything."

"Trusting God first is a wonderful choice because only He can give you that inner peace that can't be explained," Eliza placed her hand over her heart as she spoke.

"You're so right," Abigail agreed.

"We may let ourselves down, and others may let us down too; but rest assured that the King of kings will never let us down," Athens said. "I need to follow God's will and not my own. I have nothing to lose, but everything to gain." This is an opportunity for Athens to free himself from his fear of heights.

"The Truth is that everyone is afraid of something. Some people will never admit their fears, yet they can take over a person's every thought and keep them from living up to their potential," Eliza explained. "Everyone's fears are different, but we all have them. At some point, we all need to face our own fears and try to overcome them."

Abigail bit her bottom lip. "I'm afraid of the dark."

"I'm claustrophobic," said Addison.

"What's that?" Athens asked with a puzzled look on his face.

"I start feeling anxious and I can't breathe when I get into small, tight places," Addison confessed. "Not to change the subject, but getting to experience one of the greatest wonders of the world will be pretty amazing."

"Anyone can conquer their fear," Eliza said encouragingly.

"You can do it. I believe in you!" Abigail said as she tried to cheer him up with a smile.

As they began their march to the monument of *Christ The Redeemer,* Abigail put her hand on Athens' shoulder. "It's by faith that you have taken steps forward to trust God, knowing that you have been righteously chosen. You've already proven that you have faith like Daniel in the lion's den." Abigail turned to Addison. "Have you ever heard of Daniel and the lion's den?"

"No."

"No harm came to Daniel after the king's men had him thrown into a pit with ferocious lions. God appeared in the den and protected Daniel from the mouths of the lions, just like he did for us in Valley of the Kings. Remember?" Abigail said.

"What do you believe faith is?" Addison asked.

Abigail appeared to be thinking this over when Eliza jumped in. "Faith is believing in something you hope for but cannot see. Faith is like the wind; you can feel it but you can't see it. If you have faith even as small as a mustard seed, you can move mountains." She turned to Athens.

"Take the armor pieces, for example. Did you really know that they existed?" she asked.

"No, but I dreamed that they did, and now I'm wearing them," Athens whispered.

"Then by faith, you trusted God and embarked on this quest to find the armor pieces, which you did not know existed for sure. But now that you have received them by faith, your confidence in God has increased," Eliza said.

"So, when I received the shoes in the fire, it took faith to step into the flames?" Athens piped in.

"Yes, just like it did for Shadrach, Meshach, and Abednego," said Eliza.

"Who are they?" Abigail asked.

"They were three young Hebrew men who were thrown into a fiery furnace because they did not bow down to worship King Nebuchadnezzar of Babylon. They didn't get burned because God was in the fire with them. Not one hair on their heads was harmed and the ropes that bound them were burnt off. I know God will be with you too," Eliza said.

Approaching the mountain, they were in awe of its enormous size. Athens wasn't sure where to begin; he was hoping Eliza would guide them, but she was needed elsewhere on a different heavenly mission.

Abigail tugged on Athens' shirt. When he turned around, he saw a cute little old man wearing a straw hat standing beneath an umbrella on the street corner next to his vending cart selling sugar loaves. Behind the little old man were two cows, each having the number seven woven into their foreheads. The cows watched as Athens approached them.

"Ola," the little old man said as he extended his hand and offered Athens a sugar loaf. "Here you go, try some of my sugar. It's the finest in the land." Athens extended his hand toward the little old man.

"It's made of local sugar beets. It's very sweet and good to eat. We grow the finest sugar in all the world right here."

"I'll try some," Abigail quickly offered. Athens handed her the sugarloaf and became intrigued by the two cows with the number seven on their foreheads so he asked, "what's up with the cows?" I've never seen one with an actual number imprinted on its head and you have two of them." He told them the story of how the cows were a miracle sent by God as a warning of what was yet to come. Abigail ate bite after bite of the sugar loaf as they listened. Athens stared at her.

Abigail's cheeks turned cherry red. "Oops, sorry." She broke pieces off the loaf and gave some to her friends. "After all, that's what friends are for," she added.

Addison smiled and took a bite of the sugar loaf. "We're on our way to the top of the monument. Can you please tell us the best way to get there?" he asked the little old man. He quickly pointed them in the direction to the far east side of the mountain.

"Thank you, Sir. We'll be on our way now," Athens said as they walked away. A bit hesitant, walking toward the mountain, the fear of climbing began to sink in again. Athens' face turned as white as a ghost. Addison gripped his shoulder. "Keep walking by faith, my friend. Don't look back."

"When you get to the top, you won't believe the view. It's spectacular!" yelled the little old man.

"I believe in you," Abigail whispered as she patted Athens' back.

Athens said a silent prayer for courage before venturing up the mountain. A circle of clouds formed above them and expanded across the sky, passing over their heads. A light mist fell from heaven.

Abigail held her arms above her head. "This isn't good."

The mist quickly turned into a light sprinkle that turned into a drizzle that turned into a gentle rain. Before they knew it, they were standing in the thick of it as the rain came pouring down. "Let's find shelter, and quick!" Abigail said above the roaring rain.

Giant-sized balls of ice began pounding the ground, crushing everything in sight. Each one looked like they could have easily weighed one hundred pounds judging by their size and the imprints left on the earth. "Run for your lives!" Athens yelled.

Searching high and low hoping to find shelter, they discovered a crevasse along the side of the mountain. The opening was not particularly large, but then it opened up a bit into a small cave once they were inside. They all managed to make it in and escape the fury of the hailstones.

Before long, they were joined by a curious little nighthawk that also flew in to escape the storm. She perched herself on a ledge inside the dark cave. Loud thunder and lightning crackled in the sky as they squeezed in tight to avoid the storm's wrath. Addison covered his ears; He hated the loud noise of the thunder. Without warning, the rocks within the mountain began to shake and rumble. The violent hailstorm caused an avalanche and the great stones on the face of the mountain came crumbling down and fell at the mouth of the cave, barricading Athens and his friends inside.

"No one panic. I'm sure there's another way out," Athens exclaimed.

The walls seemed as if they were closing in on them. Mysterious noises were coming from within the mountain.

"I'm feeling a little claustrophobic. I don't have a good feeling about this," Addison's voice cracked.

"I don't like being squashed into small dark places either. It makes me feel panicky and anxious!" Abigail's bottom lip quivered as she reached out to grab ahold of Athens' arm.

Athens sighed. What could he say or do to help?

"All we need is a little faith to move mountains. Don't forget, we're here to find the Shield of Faith, aren't we? Don't let a dark space paralyze your thoughts; think positive thoughts. Why don't we sing a song?" Athens suggested. "Abigail, you lead."

"Seriously?" she paused.

"Yeah, I think it'll help."

She twisted her hair for a moment, then lowered her hand and started singing. Standing side by side, her soft voice was soothing and was carried throughout the cave. As the others joined in, the spirit of their voices moved together as one in perfect harmony. Their singing completely transformed their outlook and soothed their hearts and minds.

***

Feeling more confident, Abigail let go of Athens' arm and leaned against a wall that slowly began to move. Unsure of her footing, trying not to fall, she realized the wall opened into a secret passage that led into an underground tunnel.

"Stay close!" Abigail cried. "I can't see a thing."

"Don't worry," Addison said. "I'm here."

A golden lampstand with seven candles mysteriously appeared on a ledge in the darkness where they were standing. Addison picked it up as Athens opened his backpack to get the globe.

The little nighthawk followed closely behind, and finally spoke, "Can I come too? I'm scared. I can't find my family and the storm is so loud."

Abigail smiled. "Of course, you can come."

"Thank you. I'm Natalie, by the way."

"I'm Abigirl, I mean Abigail and these are my friends Athens and Addison."

Addison looked from Athens to Abigail and then to the nighthawk. His eyebrows furrowed together. "Aren't either of you a little shocked? I mean, the bird is *talking!*"

Athens laughed. "Natalie isn't the first talking animal we've met on this journey.

I guess I'm used to it by now."

Addison scratched the back of his head.

"What happened to your family, Natalie?" Abigail asked.

Natalie looked away and then softly said. "My family didn't want to listen to me when I told them about the massive storm. They stayed home, but I decided to leave. Now more than ever, I miss my great-grandpa's big hugs, his funny stories, and my Yia Yia's wonderful treehouse garden."

"I'm sorry," Abigail said as she petted her. "I'm sure the storm will be over soon, and we'll find a way out, somehow."

"This is bizarre weather we're having. It doesn't look like we'll be doing much sightseeing today," Addison said with disappointment.

While walking down the path that Abigail discovered, Natalie perched on Athens' shoulder. "I can tell there's something special about you, but I can't quite put my beak on it. What brings you to Brazil? Are you here for the festival? We have the greatest carnival on earth, where everything comes to life right on the streets, just like magic. My favorite is the cupcake competition."

"I'd love to have one of those right about now," said Abigail.

"Well, I get the breadcrumbs right off the table and believe me, they're delicious," Natalie chirped.

"I'm so hungry I could eat an elephant," Abigail suggested. "However, if you must know the truth, we're on a global mission. Right now, we're in search of a sacred armor piece called the Shield of Faith. Once we find it, we'll continue on our journey until we get to the land of milk and honey in Israel. Would you like to come with us? We'd love to have a bird's-eye view." Abigail giggled.

"I've never been on an adventure before, but maybe it would be good for me." After pondering the thought, Natalie tweeted, "Sure, I'd love to go with you. You can count me in, that is, if we ever find our way out of here."

Addison exhaled a deep breath.

"Are you okay?" Athens asked.

"Well, if you really want to know the truth, I don't have a family to speak of. That's why I'm on my way to Israel. I want to find my Jewish roots."

"I sort of understand what you're going through. I lost my parents when I was younger and now, I live with my grandmother," Abigail said.

Athens had never been separated from his family until now so he understood the desire to want to be with them. He closed his eyes and imagined what it would be like living in the King's mansion filled with the love of his family and friends. It would truly be great to live a life free from fear, worry and pain.

Everyone stood in silence just long enough to hear music coming up from beneath their feet. The ground gently rumbled, and their feet vibrated as the music grew louder and louder.

"What could it be?" Athens asked. It was the most amazing sound he had ever heard. He moved carefully, listened closely, and followed the music. The others followed behind. Waves of harps, strings, violins, and horns all played majestically together.

Natalie flew ahead and twittered, "Follow me." After climbing over some gigantic rocks, she led them between two huge boulders with barely enough room to spare. The stone walls were dark, wet and slippery, causing the group to tumble on top of each other like a pile of bowling pins. Getting up was not easy. The stones were extremely slimy, and the walls were nearly impossible to hang on to. Finally, they stood in one accord and pushed through to the other side. They could see a short tunnel that opened into a small cavern. They walked over to it and noticed a small stream of water that ran along the wall and flowed over some of the stones they had just climbed. They followed a narrow path in a little farther and found the stream flowing from a delightful pool of glowing water. The pool was so vibrant and refreshing, the water seemed to be living.

"What do you think the water is used for?" Addison asked.

Before anyone answered, candles were mysteriously lit and filled the entire room. Addison followed Abigail to have a look around. A knight in masterful armor stood at the end of the cavern behind an altar. Athens' eyes widened. It was quite extraordinary.

Athens tapped his finger against his chin. *The shield must be somewhere nearby.* He approached the altar and knelt down to pray when Natalie perched beside him fluffing her feathers.

Athens lifted his head. Low and behold... the shield's reflection shone brightly in Natalie's eyes.

Athens stood and moved toward the shield. He studied the four images engraved on it, wondering what they could possibly mean: There was the face of a man, a lion's head, an ox, and an eagle.

Like a ray from heaven, Eliza magically appeared. "Athens, you have found the shield, congratulations! These images are symbols of God, and each one has great meaning. The lion represents supreme strength; the man – wisdom; the Ox - lowly service; the eagle – heavenliness and divinity. Your faith has brought you here, and now it's time to take up the shield and head to the top of the mountain to conquer your fear."

Eliza opened a passageway and led them to the top of the mountain that the giant statue of Christ The Redeemer stood upon.

"I can do this. I got this," Athens said shakily, as he moved from the center of the mountain top toward the edge. Before he looked at the countryside below, he felt the urgency to pray. "Please Jesus, remove my fear and give me strength and peace in my heart." Just as he opened his eyes a cool breeze blew across his face. His stomach was uneasy.

He took in a deep breath that stirred his faith and courage. Then he looked over the edge. A wave of relief flooded through him. He'd just conquered his fear.

His friends rushed over. "You did it!" Abigail said. "And you helped us conquer our fears too!"

"Thanks, man." Addison patted him on the back.

Athens grinned. He raised both hands up toward heaven and shouted from the edge of the mountain, "I can do all things through Jesus Christ who strengthens me!"

Addison's lips parted. "Who's this Jesus you're talking about? I don't know Him."

"This great monument that we are standing under is of Jesus. The Son of God and man. Someday, the whole world will know Him and call Him by name. He came into the world in human form to save us from our sins. To this day His Spirit is alive. He still performs miracles and changes lives just like He did when He walked the earth over two thousand years ago."

Athens was strengthened and filled with the anointing power of Jesus Christ. "Whoever believes and trusts in Him will have the gift of eternal life in heaven. Our job as believers is to share the message of hope, love, and forgiveness, and tell others about His goodness and mercy. Everyone has sinned and we all need a Savior to forgive us."

"What is sin?" Addison asked.

Athens shifted his weight from one foot to the other and looked at Abigail, then turned back to Addison. How was he supposed to answer? Before long, Athens spoke. "Sin is doing anything outside of the will of God—including most things you know you shouldn't do like stealing, lying, or cheating. Hurting people on purpose is a sin. If you don't tell the truth, you are deceiving yourself and others. God doesn't like it when we choose to do the wrong things. It puts our hearts in a bad place and causes our relationship with Jesus to be weakened.

All sin has consequences, though each sin may have a different consequence. It may not happen right away, but everything eventually comes back full circle."

Athens drew a circle on the ground with his finger, then looked up intently. "God wrote the Law for us to live by, but it was too hard to follow, so He chose to send His only Son into the world to help us. Jesus paid the price for our sins with His life by shedding His blood on the cross so that someday when we die, we get to go to heaven."

Next, Athens drew a cross in the soil. Abigail knelt beside him to listen. "Those who believe the truth about God's Son and allow Him to work in them and through them, will be forgiven and inherit the Kingdom of Heaven."

Eliza chimed in. "It's a privilege to get to go to heaven. Someday, every knee will bend, and every head will bow before the throne of God. Those who deny Him and plot to do evil will not inherit God's Kingdom but will be separated from Him forever. Separation from God is not only separation from His presence, but also His benefits. Since all good things come from God, outside of God no good thing can exist. This means that without Him there is no love, joy, peace, hope, or fulfillment... only darkness, anguish, and despair. God desires for everyone to abide with Him forever and live with His blessing, but He will not force anyone to do so. Some may dislike God's way of doing things, but by refusing His standards, they also refuse His benefits. It's God's principles that produce His blessing."

"I don't want to live separated from Christ," Addison said, wiping the sweat from his brow. "It sounds miserable."

Athens nodded his head to agree. "That's why it's so important to let God's Holy Spirit work through you. Without Him it's impossible to achieve God's standards; but with Him working in you, His standards will become natural to you. With the Belt of Truth, the Breastplate of Righteousness, and the Gospel Shoes of Peace, I am equipped to share the good news and to be a good example for others to follow. All you have to do is believe in Christ, turn away from your sin, and let Him work through you so that you can enter His Kingdom and have your name written in the Lamb's Book of Life. Once we admit the truth, that we are sinners, and believe in our hearts that Jesus came into the world and died for our sins, and confess it with our lips, then we are saved from God's wrath."

"Can we pray and ask Him right now?" Addison pleaded as he crossed his arms and placed one hand under his chin.

"Yeah, let's ask Him now!" Abigail asked while biting her nails.

"Sure! there's no time like the present," Athens said. They joined hands. "Lord Jesus, the Son of the everlasting Father, please fill our hearts and lives with your Holy Spirit. Forgive us for our sins. Fill us with Your love, forgiveness, and mercy. Reveal Yourself to us in a mighty way so that we will do Your will and not our own. Thank you for loving us unconditionally and for helping us overcome our fears, doubts, anxiety and worries. In Jesus Holy name, Amen. The three of them looked up into the sky and stared into the heavens in awe as they witnessed a shooting star streak across the sky. Eliza's heart was bursting with joy as she stretched out her hands. She looked down and noticed Abigail's necklace. "The necklace you're wearing is a symbol of Jesus. He has shown His love for you by revealing the cross."

"Oh wow, you're right. I'm so blessed, thank you!" Abigail said while stroking her necklace.

Eliza gave her a radiant smile before fading out. Athens led his trio of friends down the mountainside to make their way back to the rock. Standing back-to-back with locked arms Natalie perched herself on Athens' shoulder. Without hesitation, he spoke the words, then they spun around, and instantly disappeared without a trace.

CHAPTER 5

Defeating the Enemy

HELMET OF SALVATION

Deception Island, Antarctica

Athens and his friends appeared, dressed in warm pants and winter coats, ready to explore when Eliza entered the atmosphere like a ray of sunshine.

"There's no other place on Earth quite like Antarctica," she exclaimed. "It's the coldest and darkest place in the world. Beyond the icebergs and freezing snowy weather, there are many hidden treasures that have been kept secret until now. You'll soon discover how this volcanic island got its name. The mountain sides have deep dredges in them that were carved out by hot lava that spewed out of the volcano and collided with the ocean waves. This gives it a very mysterious look. Did you know that it's dark nearly six months out of the year here at the South Pole?"

Abigail shivered as she rubbed her nose. "Wait, What? I'm glad we won't be here for that long."

"Living in darkness with barely any light for months at a time would feel like torture," Natalie tweeted as her feathers shook in the frigid cold air.

"There's no way I could even imagine living in darkness every day. That would definitely be depressing," Addison said as he shook his head, then placed his hands in his pockets to try to keep warm.

Athens looked around and was intrigued by the strange-looking mossy weeds growing on the ground. "Are those edible?"

Eliza replied, "Nothing much grows here, besides Pearlwort and hair grass plants, because of the freezing temperatures. That's one reason why few people live here. For decades, not a single rumor of volcanic activity was found on the island until now. Something very strange is happening. There's a supermassive black hole that keeps spreading throughout the region. No one knows where it came from or why it's here. Some people believe that the black hole was caused by something from outer space, called kryptonite matter, that fell from the sky, forming the hole. Rumor has it that it could be a portal used by fallen angels and their offspring to travel back and forth from one dimension to another, allowing evil activity to wreak havoc on Earth."

"That sounds crazy, but my dad used to tell me stories about the Nephilim hybrids, who were the children of the fallen angels. I hope we don't run into any of them while we're here," Athens replied.

"Look over there," Abigail was intrigued. "Sled mushers with their dogs. It looks like they're getting ready for a race.

I think it would be cool to watch them run through the snow!"

"The mushers must have complete focus if they wish to succeed. However, the dogs also play an important role; They are amazing animals and work hard as a team. They're completely obedient and devoted to their masters. I read it in a book back home." Athens said while rubbing his hands together to keep warm.

Eliza quickly chimed in, "The mushers must remain clear-minded, light-hearted, and quick on their feet; staying focused is crucial to the task. In the same way, Athens must be completely in unison with God's mission if he plans on finishing the quest on time." She turned and gave Abigail a stern look.

Abigail's cheeks flushed. "Right. Okay, let's go."

They all walked along the frigid shoreline looking for clues on where to find the Helmet of Salvation, when an enormous, human sized penguin waddled over to them. "My word, you boys are a couple of handsome gems." Speaking to Athens and Addison, of course. "Your eyes are as bright as the morning sun and twinkle like the evening stars, and your hair is as shiny as a midsummer's eve. I think I'm falling in love already. May I add that your friends are as lovely as the light on a moonlit sky."

Eliza's blue eyes twinkled as she raised her eyebrows.

Athens and Abigail blushed, and Addison's grin spread from ear to ear.

While she was speaking, a gorgeous young lady wearing warm gloves and an Eskimo coat approached them from the village. Standing on the ocean bank she asked in a calm, soothing voice, "What gives us the honor of your presence? My name is Diona Ardearest; this is my friend, Penelope."

Penelope quickly tried to hide her face behind Diona. She seemed a little embarrassed about being too outspoken.

Athens introduced himself and his friends and was about to share his quest when Abigail interrupted and asked, "How on earth did you get to be so big?" staring at the penguin. "You're ginormous! If you don't mind me saying so."

Natalie twittered. "I was about to ask the same thing."

Penelope stood tall and proud, then replied, "I inherited the genes from my prehistoric ancestors. They were the same monumental size as I am. My family comes in all different shapes, colors, and sizes. I love them all. I also love ice-sculpting with my beak, in case you wanted to know. It's very rewarding, except when my tongue gets stuck to the ice." Everyone chuckled.

"Honestly, there are some perks to being large. For instance, being this tall helps me see from a distance, and it's especially nice when I'm on the ice or when I'm about to dive into the ocean to catch some fish. Have you ever seen a crucifix catfish before?" she asked, but before anyone could answer, she continued. "I happen to have some over here. Come take a look."

When Penelope took a breath, Diona took over the conversation. "Every year fishermen come from all over the world to enter a world renown fishing competition. Last year my grandfather won first place for catching the largest crucifix catfish, and he was only in a small canoe. There's some places even a yacht can't go." Addison laughed.

The crucifix catfish bones were laid out on the snow. Its skull had jagged edges and was thick in the middle. On the bottom of the skull, you could almost see a face etched out of the top-center portion with arms stretched out on both sides, and the legs were aiming down, just like the image of Jesus on the cross.

Athens stared in fascination. "What an amazing skeletal structure. Its brilliant!"

"When you shake the bones and hear a rattle in the breastplate, it'll bring you good luck," Penelope said as she picked up the bones and rattled them. "That's so cool," Addison held out his hand to shake the bones.

"We just came from Brazil, where Christ The Redeemer Monument is located. This is an amazing confirmation of His existence," Athens said in a high-pitched voice. "I'm searching for a unique helmet that belongs to the great King Elohim."

"What helmet, and who is King Elohim?" Diona turned the palms of her hands up in the air as she inquired.

"The Helmet of Salvation has supernatural powers and was crafted in the heavenly realms. It's one of six armor pieces that I need, and so far, I have four of them."

"The past four days, we've been traveling all around the world. We just came from Brazil in South America. We'll soon be on the other side of the world in America,

searching in a place called Yosemite National Park, in California," Abigail said.

"All the armor pieces work together to create supernatural elements of power and protection used to defeat evil. Once I find them all and take them to the King of Israel, we will inherit a king's reward and have the gift of Eternal Life. It will forever change our lives. I need to find the helmet before it's too late. Do you happen to know where I can find it?" Athens asked.

Diona and Penelope looked at each other with raised brows. Athens was waiting for an answer when Diona looked at him with her piercing brown eyes and said, "My Papou, I mean my grandpa, just shared a story with us a few days ago. It stuck out in my mind because he mentioned something about an old volcano with dark treasures, a map, and a supernatural helmet. My grandfather is Greek and wants to make sure that his stories and traditions are passed down from generation to generation, keeping them alive for all the ages to come. He's always telling us new stories, but often repeats the old ones; We just thought they were old wise' tales and enjoyed listening to them. I didn't believe there was much truth to them until now." Diona continued, "I remember him telling us about the helmet's significance and how it can change the way people think and behave. He spoke of a dark cave, and how it could play tricks on people's minds."

Eliza raised her hand in the air, "The helmet has the power to protect a person's mind from deception. Knowing the truth and seeing the difference between right and wrong is wonderful, but merely knowing is not enough.

The power comes from doing the right thing, especially when you don't want to."

"If you trust the guidance of God's Holy Spirit, you can have hope when all hope seems to be lost." Athens moved in close.

"I have to be completely honest with you," Diona explained. "Anyone brave enough to go in there must first be aware of the dangers. There are two kinds of wars; physical and spiritual. Both are battles between light and dark, good and evil. It's up to you to figure out which is which. By the way, I can get my Papou's map for you, perhaps it will help."

"That would be great," Athens replied. "Oh, wait," he whispered, remembering that he had his 3D onyx globe with him. He pulled it out of his backpack to get a glimpse of the cave, but it didn't give him the vision he expected. Instead, an image of heaven appeared, and all eyes gazed upon its beauty. "We may need the map after all." He shrugged his shoulders.

"I can meet you in town and give it to you in about an hour, but first, I need to give you a few tips," Diona tilted her head to the side and winked. "Get on your knees and pray. Many great kings and mighty men have been led to their doom by worshiping the idols found in these caves, so be wary."

Eliza chimed in, "The cave which Diona speaks of leads deep into the bowels of the earth, where great chambers of treasure lay with a dark curse upon it. There are many vile creatures that dwell in those deep places. These creatures take great pleasure in deceiving others and taking possession of their thoughts. That's why you must be diligent about guarding your mind; never allow your thoughts to turn against you, causing doubt, fear, worry, or anxiety. It's a trick these foul creatures use to lead you astray and rob you of your God given free will. They want to steal your soul. If you do not resist the urge, your mind will be consumed in darkness." Eliza paced around them. Athens' heart pounded rapidly. He had no intensions of being deceived.

"I remember my father telling me stories about the Nephilim from one of his ancient books called *The Book of Enoch;* They are fearsome creatures," Athens said.

Penelope replied, "Deception Island is in the shape of a U and draws in unsuspecting souls to it with its magnetic, mystical forces that lay within the volcano walls. People have come in search of riches and Scientists have come here searching for portals to other universes. They never leave the island the same way they came, if they leave at all. Most disappear and are never seen again." They all stood listening, like frozen statues.

"Wow, that's scary! I don't mean to sound dumb, but what are Nephilim?" Natalie asked with a screeched voice as her beak chattered together.

Diona replied, "They're the hybrid children of humans and fallen angels; they're entirely wicked beings."

"According to my dad, they can transform themselves into almost anything. We must not be fooled by their outward beauty; it's merely an illusion." Said Athens.

Then Eliza gave them one final alert. "You will encounter many alluring treasures in the cave, but don't be deceived, all is cursed but the Helmet of Salvation. Whatever you do, touch only what you were sent to retrieve. The Nephilim will try to use their powers to keep you from leaving and imprison you in the deep places of the world."

Abigail noticeably swallowed hard as her eye's grew wide with fear.

Diona encouraged them. "Be strong, be brave, be alert, and above all else, use self-control. This is no ordinary cavern. The moment you yield your mind to the enchantment of the cave, all may be lost."

"Oh dear!" Abigail pleaded. "This may be a problem for me."

Eliza stated, "Their power and beauty will make it nearly impossible for you to turn away. Only a true believer can overcome the obstacles that lay ahead. The secret is to keep your eyes centered on the truth and protect your heart, mind, and body, so you can press on to the prize ahead of you and not give in to temptations in front of you." Eliza opened up her hands and magically showed them a golden relic inlayed with rubies and sapphires. She closed her hands and in a flash it vanished.

Eliza was forbidden to go into the cave to help Athens, so she gave him a menorah candlelight to guide them in the dark.

Athens handed the light stand to Abigail, "Don't forget, I have the globe that my parents gave me."

Abigail gave an exalted laugh, "At least now I'm somewhat armed."

"I, uh... I think I'll stay behind," said Addison.

Natalie flew off of Athens' shoulder and landed on Addison's. "I'll keep you company. I wouldn't want you to feel lonely."

Athens shrugged. He didn't want to risk their lives anyway. "That's fine. If we don't come back in a few hours, send someone to look for us."

Eliza spoke to the group, "The best thing we can do for Athens and Abigail is to pray for them. Pray that they'll escape the many snares that have been set before them." Eliza turned back to Athens. She held a unique and precious stone in her hand called Eilat that was carved into the shape of a gigantic egg. "This came from King Solomon's Mine and is the only one of its kind in the world. You must put this in place of the helmet when the helmet is presented to you. This will be a true test of your character; to be able to do God's will and not your own is the ultimate test." She handed Athens the precious stone.

"I hope that you understand the importance of it," Eliza said.

Penelope gave Athens a giant hug, "I hope you return safe and sound to join us later this evening."

"I sure hope so too," Athens replied.

Diona quickly left to go get her Papou's map. Everyone else headed over to watch Penelope's ice-sculpting exhibition.

When Diona returned, she gave Abigail the map. Athens took another look into his globe. If only he could catch a glimpse of what lay ahead... but it wouldn't reveal anything to him. Why wasn't it working?

"It's not a crystal ball," Eliza stated. "It's a way for you to see what you have to look forward to, and also to strengthen you for the tasks ahead. You can track where you've been. Beyond that, it may provide light in dark places. You know we don't always get what we want, but God always gives what we need."

Athens was disappointed by her answer, but accepted the truth.

"By the way," Diona mentioned as she peered up at the sky, "I thought you should know, there will be a total lunar eclipse tonight and it's believed that something extraordinary will happen around midnight."

"Yes, it's a natural phenomenon that occurs when the sun, earth, and moon are all three in total alignment," Eliza confirmed as she twirled her hands into the shape of a ball and created a miniature moonbeam. When she released it from her hands it floated into the atmosphere.

"It's a sign from God that something big is about to happen," Athens said.

Diona gazed at the moonbeam, "Yes, it's an extremely rare occurrence."

"Maybe it's your lucky night; you're going to need it," Addison suggested.

"No luck needed," Athens said. "This is our God appointed destiny."

They all gazed upon the mountain smoke lingering beneath the moonlit sky.

Athens and Abigail departed with the ancient map and headed down a path to discover the volcano's secret entrance. They trekked through the thick snow as more flakes fell on their coats and covered their heads in white. A huge rumbling noise broke out, and the ground began to vibrate, throwing them off balance.

Athens and Abigail fled for cover, hoping to escape the volcano's fury. They entered a dark and dreary cave.

Abigail used the menorah lamp to look at the map, but the light blew out. The air was thick and musty. They began to hear a loud outlandish noise sweeping through the cave. A colony of bats flew in from another room.

"Yikes!" Abigail screamed as she swatted at the bats with the menorah and ducked her head in fear of getting bitten.

Athens put his shield in front of them and immediately closed his eyes and prayed, "Jesus, please protect us."

A golden aura of light surrounded them in a bubble and kept the bats from coming near them. The bats circled over their heads, trying to find a way in, but kept bouncing off the shield. Some of them hit the walls, some of them hit the ground, and the rest fled back to wherever they came from.

Athens scrunched his nose. "Where were they going?" He looked over at Abigail who had her eyes closed tight. "You can open your eyes now, they're gone."

"We won't be trapped down here forever, will we?" Abigail cried out when she bit her nail so hard that it drew blood.

Athens held her hand and covered their heads with his shield as they scurried through the dimly lit cave. The rough walls of the cave glittered because of the protruding gemstones.

Abigail let go of Athens' hand and felt along the wall as she passed by. Some of the gems were loose and fell out as she touched them. She quickly picked them up and put them in her pockets. Before long, she had plucked out many brilliant gems of every shape, size, and color. Layer upon layer of precious diamonds, sparkling sapphires, rubies of fire, and stunning green emeralds were set in the walls of the cave.

Athens stopped mid-step. Was she losing her mind? Was she actually pocketing the gems?

Before he could consider it for too long, he heard a faint noise and looked up. Three volcanic tubes appeared before them and lead straight up. Where had the noise come from?

Athens quietly followed the tube on his right. A reflection came from the walls inside. He squinted through the darkness. What was it? He stepped closer to get a better view. It was a series of glow worms only found in the deepest parts of the earth. They moved and shimmered in the dim light.

He took a step back and gasped, "What an extraordinary discovery." A message inlayed with diamonds was engraved in the wall and read, *Behold, the hand of God is upon you. Only one with a pure heart will inherit the Kingdom of God.*

This was an incredible find. Athens looked ahead, down the tube, and could see a brightly illuminated object. Could that be the helmet? Advancing toward it, he suddenly froze, and could hardly believe his eyes. A still, quiet voice filled his mind that said, *The helmet will keep your mind clear from deception and protect your thoughts from ungodly thinking. It will keep you hidden, so others will not see you.*

Eliza's words about the Eilat stone came back all-too quickly. His life and the lives of many were depending on it.

The brilliant stone felt extremely heavy as its beauty glistened in his hands. If he kept it for himself, it could make him rich. But should he disobey God? Was his willpower to do the right thing greater than his desire for money?

Athens reached his hands out to touch the helmet but hesitated. Was he having second thoughts? He'd come so far. But he couldn't reach it; the helmet began glimmering as it ascended from its pedestal. Suspended in midair, he watched the helmet begin to descend, eventually resting upon his head. He took the Eilat stone, and placed it on the helmet's pedestal, and then put his hands on top of the helmet. "Thank you, God, for this mighty gift."

The dazzling gems were inlayed in the helmet and totally lit up the room as they encircled Athens' head like a majestic glowing crown; there was no other helmet like it. It fit snugly as though it was meant to be his all along. It made every cell in his body tingle and he felt lighter somehow. He glanced down at his torso and suddenly let out a little yelp... He was becoming transparent! He watched as his body shimmered, then slowly faded and disappeared.

He was invisible! Athens turned around to look for Abigail, but she wasn't there.

He felt the spirit of God upon him and sensed the presence of evil everywhere, now that he was wearing the helmet. He had to find her. Had she become enticed by the enchanted gemstones?

"Abigail," he whispered. "Where are you?" Athens walked through small dark places searching for her but eventually headed back in the direction he came from.

As he continued searching for Abigail, he discovered a chamber filled with mounds of skulls and great piles of bones in dark hidden places as far as the eye could see. He quickly passed on to the next tunnel without disturbing the remains. He discovered cages with humans in them. They appeared to be filthy dirty humans sentenced to death with no hope of escape. A circle of flames separated them from Athens. There was no way to help them even if he wanted to.

Athens eventually made his way back to the mouth of the intersection between the three tunnels where he had been separated from Abigail, when a loud noise erupted from the tube next to him. Athens came out of his tunnel and proceeded a little way back into the main cavern, so that he could see what had happened in the tunnel beside him. Peering into what had apparently been the middle tunnel, Athens saw what looked like a meteor shower, appearing in the grave tunnel. He stood in shock as flashes of light formed inside the tunnel creating distorted skeletons of abominable shapes before transforming into beautiful, almost angelic, like beings by the time their feet touched the ground. They no longer appeared as wicked, demonic creatures but were transfigured by illusion. They had to be the Nephilim. "Wow, Abigail's never gonna believe this."

Abigail must have heard the noise too because a second later she peeked her head around the corner on the left. Not realizing the creatures had transformed, she stood staring at them, star struck by their beauty.

"Come on, stop gawking! Let's go before we're trapped down here forever in this God forsaken place."

"Athens? Is that you?" Abigail's voice quivered as she looked around for him. "I can't see you."

Athens took a deep breath. "I'm wearing the helmet, and it's making me invisible." Athens squeezed her hand tight before tiptoeing back through the main tunnel, but this time Abigail tripped over a string, and her arms flailed in the air. "Whoa!"

Somehow, they'd passed over it on their way in.

Athens reached out and grabbed her, pulling her to a standing position. His gaze traveled to the string, which was connected to a giant pendulum.

The blood rushed out of his face. It was a trap.

The pendulum swung back and forth like an axe. Athens pulled Abigail down as he ducked. The axe pendulum grazed the top of Athens' helmet and knocked it off.

"There you are," Abigail said. "Now I can see you. Thank God that thing didn't cut your head off."

The Nephilim creatures turned in their direction. No longer disguised with beautiful form, their vivid red, yellow, and green eyes burned with hatred. They had a ravenous look about their faces, like wild beasts. They opened their mouths and revealed nasty fangs and disfigured, razor-sharp teeth.

The earth began to shake, making all of them unsteady on their feet. As the Nephilim tried to catch their balance, Abigail and Athens ran toward the cave entrance.

Smoldering fumes began to rise up from the floor of the cave. The volcano was getting ready to erupt. Many daggers that hung from the ceiling shook loose and fell upon the Nephilim like great spears. But the Nephilim were determined not to let them escape as they drug their bodies along the hot ground grabbing at their ankles.

Athens pumped his arms, running faster.

Abigail's pace slowed as she reached for jewels, stuffing them in her coat pockets.

The ground beneath them began to split and a river of lava with flames seeped through the cracks in the ground. Athens could see the faint light of the cave entrance that was just ahead. If only they could get through, the pursuit would cease; these foul beings hate daylight.

He needed to rouse Abigail from her trance. "Run, Abigail, run!"

Athens had a brilliant idea after seeing smoke charged from the debris in the lava pit, he reached his hands behind his head and pulled out his ponytail. It was a remnant of hair he'd been hiding since childhood. It was the secret he'd kept hidden all these years. Athens bent down and picked up a mining knife he saw stemming out of the ground, and swiftly cut off his ponytail leaving only a few strands behind. Then lit the rest on fire from the lava and brimstone seeping up from the ground. The hair on his arm was singed when he felt the heat on his skin. He rose to his feet and waved the hair in front of him hoping to create a smoke screen. It worked!

Abigail finally stopped stuffing her pockets and began to run. But the extra weight slowed her down. Athens raced toward her and covered their heads with the shield as more daggers crashed down from above. Natalie the night hawk flew in and began attacking the creatures poking their eyes out. One of the Nephilim was within arm's reach and lunged toward her. Abigail quickly emptied her pockets causing the creature to stumble and fall.

A glorious wind blew in from the mouth of the cave and magnified the smoke and ashes from Athens' hair and blinded the creature.

Athens and Abigail barely made it out alive. The shaking of the mountain slowly came to a halt. They hugged when they saw Natalie fly out of the cave. Athens quickly remembered to wrap the remnant of hair he had left with a string that dangled from his shirt and tucked it away. Abigail was curious about why he had hidden it from her for so long. It was a test of obedience and trust on his part. His mother knew that someday he would be tested to serve God and today was that day.

"Let's hurry and go tell our friends about the helmet," Natalie twittered.

"The helmet is truly a masterpiece," Abigail admitted.

Natalie flew ahead to announce they were coming. As Athens and Abigail walked into the town, all eyes were on them. For no one else had ever laid eyes on the helmet before now.

"The helmet!" Penelope cried. "It's so grandiose!"

"You have it! I can't believe it. It's truly a vision of greatness," Diona said as she clasped her hands together.

"How did you escape?" asked Addison as he raced toward them.

"With God's help, all things are possible," Athens replied. "God will always direct us in the way we should go, if we choose to pay attention. I give Him all the honor, glory, and praise." Athens held the helmet up high for all to see.

The band started playing as they walked over to sit down near a bon fire, hoping to grab a bite to eat. Diona sat them next to her papou as honored guests.

"Welcome," he said, offering them some hot chocolate as he gazed at the sight of the helmet in total amazement. "It's truly a remarkable helmet. You are very blessed."

"Yes, indeed," Athens responded. "Thank you, Sir."

Frowning, Abigail lowered her chin to her chest. Something was amiss.

"What's wrong?" Athens asked.

"I'm starting to feel anxious. I can still see the demonic creatures as if they're right in front of me." She dug her heels into the ground. "How can I get rid of the memory of their grotesque, razor-sharp teeth?"

Athens gave her the helmet to wear to protect her mind. "Remember, redirect your thinking to good things, and picture something else in your mind."

"Look, a delicious plate of fresh fish with a bowl of seaweed salad," shouted Penelope opening her beak.

Athens' mouth watered. He was starving. "It looks delicious."

Diona handed him the largest plate of food. "I hope you like it."

"I've never had seaweed salad before, but I'm willing to give it a try," he chuckled.

Abigail stared at the plate.

"What are you thinking about now, Abigail?" he asked.

"My thoughts have completely changed." She took the helmet off and placed it in Athens' backpack for safekeeping.

Remembering to say a quick prayer, Athens thanked God for all their blessings before wiping his plate clean.

"Look, the moon is turning scarlet red!" Diona cried. "The eclipse is happening!" She pointed to the moon.

Everyone cheered. They all headed over to the giant telescopes.

"What a vision. The full moon is completely red and so large you can almost reach out and touch it." A moment later the clouds concealed the moon and blocked their view. "Oh no, I hope it returns soon." Diona moaned. A few minutes later Abigail began to dance around the starlight beneath the moonlit sky as the moon reappeared.

"God has truly blessed us tonight," Addison added as he watched Abigail dancing.

Penelope spoke and insisted that Athens and his friends stay a bit longer to watch the ice-skating show.

"We really do need to be going," Athens said.

"Diona has a surprise for you. She's our featured entertainer and wanted to keep it a secret. It's a victory celebration in your honor! No one has ever done what you've done tonight," Penelope said.

"Yes, you're the first ever to retrieve the helmet and live to tell about it," said Papou.

Abigail handed Papou his map. "Thank you so much for letting us borrow it, we won't be needing it anymore."

Athens and his friends followed the crowd as they began making their was over to the town's arena, which very much resembled a large ice-skating rink with stone bleachers. All eyes watched Diona as she gracefully glided across the ice. She had three small, beautiful birds of magnificent color perched on her shoulder. The stunning birds took flight and twirled in the air above her head. What a lovely vision it was, watching their graceful moves. Diona was absolutely breathtaking too. Her arms and legs swayed back and forth like an elegant angel gently floating by. Seven more birds flew in to join her, fluttering about her as they danced in unison to the sound of the music.

A gentle snow fell on her nose and her eyelashes. She used it to her advantage while dancing beneath the moonlight. She began singing as she spun around in circles. "Snowflakes, snowflakes, lovely little snowflakes."

The snowflakes were a wondrous sight as Diona gracefully skated through them while twirling around on the ice. The reflection of the brightly colored birds on the ice began shooting radiant beams of shaded light into the sky, causing a magical rainbow effect. Streaks of rainbow danced through the air. Beautiful prisms touched down right in the center of the arena as Diona skated through them. She looked stunning with the lights floating all around her. It was a vision of heaven on earth.

"It's like the Aurora Borealis in Alaska. It is enchanting, indeed," Abigail added.

When the music slowed down, Diona's friends from the village joined her on the ice and formed a single line. They all skated in different directions creating spectacular movements and jumps. Everyone clapped and cheered for them.

Athens and his friends enjoyed their time together but knew it was time to mush off to the next continent. They wished their new friends farewell and hoped to see them again someday.

Diona and Penelope gave Athens and his friends something special to remember them by—they had handmade colorful beaded friendship bracelets. Each color has a special meaning to it and was listed on the little card that it came with.

As they headed back to the stone, Athens shook the snow off his coat as he remembered a small lighthouse they'd passed along the way. Natalie perched herself on Addison's shoulder. Finally making it back to the rock. The trio of friends locked arms and stood back-to-back. Then Athens whispered, "Guide me in Your truth and teach me Your ways, oh Lord, for You are my God, my Savior, my hope is in You all day long."

Instantly, they were transported to the United States, wearing American clothing, ready and united to take on whatever comes their way.

CHAPTER 6

A Strange and Unusual Phenomenon

THE SWORD OF THE SPIRIT

Yosemite National Park, California

"**W**ow, I think I've died and gone to heaven!" Stepping off the rock into America was quite a thrill. Athens and his friends were captivated by the view.

Eliza twirled into the atmosphere like a guiding light. "I see you've gained another piece of the armor."

Athens looked out at the surrounding scenery and replied, "Yes, each of the pieces are truly glorious and their powers are remarkable. I'm feeling more confident with each step I take toward my destiny. I know the battle is far from over, but my vision of meeting the King grows stronger every day." They stood near the base of a giant waterfall and watched as the sun was setting into the horizon.

Eliza gestured at the falls. "Deep within the forest is one of God's wonderous creations. There's a phenomenon that occurs in the midst of the woods; it lays in the valley

102

between those tree tops and mountain peaks ahead. You can hear the sound of the rushing waterfall flowing down into an enchanting place with acres of delightful creatures." She placed her hand next to her ear, as she listened. "Bridal Veil Falls is a treasured spot, noted for its grandeur, ageless beauty. By day, you can hear the sweet melodies of chirping birds, humming insects, and nature's wondrous sounds. By night, it's called Yosemite Firefall and you can see the fantastic illumination of the sun beaming into the falls, making them appear as if they were burning with red flames. Only those fortunate enough to come here during the right time of year will ever get to experience its true beauty. People travel from near and far to experience its natural artistry. This curious phenomenon occurs when the cold mountain air interacts with the last rays of sunlight just after sunset. During the right hour, waves of light come down from heaven and shoot across the sky at just the right speed, at just the right angle, and at just the right time. This magnificent phenomenon faithfully appears around the same time every year."

Eliza's voice dropped to a whisper. "There's something else you should know. Ages ago, in this very forest, giants once dwelt. If you listen closely, you might even hear the echoing sound of the giants snoring who lay sleeping beneath the tall sequoia trees of ages past. These creatures were of a wicked and mighty race. They could uproot trees and move massive stones with their bare hands." Their eyes began to look around. She continued. "These horrific giants crept into the villages late at night and stole children who were sleeping among their families and gave them to their idol gods as human sacrifices during the bewitching hour. They threw the children's bones into an open fire, then once the bones became red hot embers, they poured them out over the waterfall to imitate the red glowing river, mocking the natural beauty that God had created.

Athens and his friends didn't like the sound of that story at all.

Athens eyes peered off into the woods after Eliza departed.

***

They decided to build a fire and huddled together, hoping to forget about the thought of monstrous giants.

"Why not sing a song," Abigail suggested when a little glimmer of light showed up beside them. It was a tiny, friendly firefly.

"Who are you?" Athens asked, knowing of course, he was in an enchanted forest where anything was possible.

"My name is Zeek, short for Ezekiel. I'm a lightning bug and I'm here to help. I can keep you warm and provide plenty of light throughout the night."

"Yes, that would be great, but … "Athens chewed on the inside of his cheek. He didn't want to offend the little bug. "How can you provide that much light when you're so small? And I thought you were called a firefly"

"I may be small, but you might be surprised. Yes, some call us fireflies, but we are one in the same. The God of the Universe also has different names."

Just then an owl hooted in a nearby tree.

Abigail shuddered. "It's a little scary out here, we sure could use Him right about now."

Zeek continued, "God is also called Yeshua, Yahweh, El Shaddai and many more.

"I'm a guardian of the forest and I carry the light of hope with me. The forest can be quite dangerous with wild beasts and creatures that lurk in the shadows. I have a large family that can help keep you safe." Zeek took flight. "I'll be back."

A spark of hope ignited in Athens' heart. At least Zeek promised to return with his family. That would provide some comfort throughout the night.

Addison and Natalie gathered more sticks and twigs before tossing them into the fire pit.

Athens moved closer to the fire and rubbed his hands together, while Natalie sat on the edge of the tree stump gazing into the flames. Suddenly, a series of crackling and popping noises arose from the flames and formed into images. First, the face of a roaring lion, then a soaring eagle, and finally, a raging bear. Athens and his friends were in total awe as they gazed into the flames. The fire glowed against their faces in the dark. The animals looked as if they were revealing their own legend by mere appearance.

Suddenly, a seven-headed ten-horned dragon formed out of the burning flames. It stared right at Athens. Tingles shot up and down his spine. It looked a lot like the dragon from his dream. *"Please don't come to life. Please don't come to life,"* Abigail whispered while Addison scooted back away from the fire.

The image of the dragon vanished in the flames. Abigail blinked her eyes in disbelief.

Athens pulled out his globe and gazed into it. Hopefully, he could get another glimpse of heaven. He spun it around and around, viewing all seven continents, stopping at Israel to envision what the great city of Jerusalem would look like. A vision of the King's beautiful mansion appeared and put his mind at ease.

The campfire died down and shadows drew near as they quietly watched and waited. *Where was Zeek?* They hung their heads in disappointment nearly giving up all hope. They were getting sleepy. Athens' heavy eye lids drooped. He almost closed them completely when a light flickered beneath some fallen trees in the distance. The flicker of light turned into a beam, as a multitude of lightning bugs came flying over the hills and into the camp with Zeek leading the way. A trail of lights danced beneath the moon. Some formed lanterns as they flew through hollow trees; others created a halo around Athens' and Abigail's heads, causing them to appear as royalty. Some of them flew into the shape of wings near Addison, making him look like an angel.

Addison laughed. "What a creative, bright family you have, Zeek. They are very talented."

Zeek's light grew brighter. "Is there anything else we can do for you while we're here?"

Athens slowly said, "Well, actually, yes. We're here searching for the Sword of the Spirit. Do you have any idea where it might be?"

"The sword you speak of was forged in the heavenly realms. It's sharper than any two-edged sword and has immense power, both in the physical and spiritual world. It's on the other side of the valley beneath the crystal waterfalls, but not just anyone can claim it. It was placed there by God's hand, and only the hand of God can remove it," Zeek replied.

"I understand," said Athens. "I've been sent here to find it and prove myself worthy. King Elohim has invited me into His kingdom. If I stay true to the task and finish this quest before midnight tomorrow, my friends and I will receive a great inheritance. I must defeat and overcome the evil one and proclaim victory over the forces of darkness."

"Let's pray and hope that you find what you're looking for," Zeek said.

"Lord of lords, King of kings and creator of all things, thank you for giving us more than we deserve and for loving us as much as You do. Please put a hedge of protection around us. Give us wisdom, courage, and strength for the journey ahead. Guide us in Your Truth and teach us Your ways. We trust all things will work together for the good of Your people who glorify Your great name. Forgive us of our trespasses and forgive those who trespass against us. Lead us not into temptation but deliver us from evil. In Jesus' mighty name, Amen."

No sooner had the words left Zeek's mouth, Athens began to nod off sinking into a deep sleep. The lightning bugs made themselves at home, keeping watch over them throughout the night.

Athens was dreaming of sweeter days ahead, living a grand life in the land of milk and honey, when he realized he had a fear greater than his fear of heights. Suddenly, his fear came to life. The Earth shook beneath the ground and a tremendous noise boomed in the distance. Giants marched through the woods, uprooting the trees and overturning boulders. As soon as they saw Athens, he took off running in the opposite direction. The woods grew into a thick massive maze. Maybe they wouldn't find him in here.

But one did. A gnarly giant reached down and grabbed ahold of Athens with its giant fist and plucked him from the ground. Athens dangled upside down by his ankles. Athens beat his fists into the giant's dense skin but it had no effect. How could he get free?

The giants were taking him to their altar to be sacrificed to their gods. Athens struggled to get away, but the giant's grip was too tight. He couldn't get loose. He tried yelling for help, kicking and fighting but no words escaped his mouth. Again, he yelled for help, but no words came out. Panic seized him.

The giant's grip was so tight that Athens could barely breathe, but he would not give up. He gave one last shout and forced the air out of his mouth in a loud, clear voice. "Jesus, help me!"

The sound of his own voice woke him from his nightmare.

Athens' eyes were wide open, the palms of his hands were sweaty, and his heart was beating so fast that he could barely catch his breath. He looked around to see where he was and realized he was still in the forest, but all the lightning bugs were gone. It was nearly morning, and he was alone. *Where did everybody go?*

A rustling sound came from the branches and leaves in the trees. As it grew closer, he jumped to his feet and grabbed his backpack, prepared to run. *Was it the giants coming after him, for real this time?*

The bushes parted and Abigail and Addison strolled into the camp.

Athens put his hands on his knees. "Thank God, it's only you." His heart nearly skipped a beat. "I just had the worst nightmare ever. What were you two doing anyway?"

"We found some food for breakfast," Abigail said delightfully as she carried some over to Athens.

"What is it?" he asked.

She held out her hands. "Figs and sequoia seeds. They're quite tasty."

"I'll try some too!" Natalie chirped as she hopped on one foot while grasping some seeds with the other.

"Just think, tomorrow night we could be feasting with King Elohim. I can only imagine how wonderful the food will be!" Addison said with anticipation as he handed Athens some figs.

"All you can eat for sure; feasting for seven years, I can't wait!" Athens licked his lips while eating his figs.

"So, what was your dream about?" Abigail asked.

Athens replied, "I dreamed giants captured me and wanted to give me to their gods as a human sacrifice."

"Thank God it was only a dream," Abigail responded.

"Yes, but it could be a warning," Addison advised.

"We have to be careful. We're so close to the end of our journey. We can't let anything stop us now," Athens agreed.

They walked deeper into the forest, when a magnitude of trees swayed back and forth. The branches separated, showcasing an eclipse of gorgeous white moths that had gathered together. They formed a life-sized sword, pointing to the north.

Abigail's lips parted. "I think we should follow them."

Natalie flew over their heads trying to catch one of the moths.

Like a streak of light, Eliza appeared. "These moths are special," she said as one landed on her finger. She pointed out the black markings on their wings. "If you look closely one way, you can see a sword and shield, but when you turn them around the other way, you can see a cross and a shield."

"They're breathtaking. What are they called?" Abigail asked as she held out her hands hoping to catch one.

"The moths are called Jesus moths because of their unique markings."

"Very impressive; they remind me of the Sword of the Spirit," Athens said as one landed in the palm of his hands.

Eliza added, "The Sword works best when the Spirit of God is present in our lives, working in us, for us, and through us; it's sharper than any two-edged sword."

"God creates the most amazing things," Addison admired.

Eliza further explained that, "the Word of God breathes life into the believer and gives hope that surpasses all understanding."

A kaleidoscope of moths flew up from behind the bushes, all having the face of Jesus on the back of their wings.

"How marvelous!" Abigail gasped.

"Listen." Athens heard a faint howling noise. "Shh. It sounded like a pack of wolves that time," he said as he heard the noise again.

Natalie spread her wings and flew to the treetops to have a look around. She came back shivering and couldn't speak. Addison climbed up a tree to see if he could find what frightened her. In the distance, a large, dark, wolf-like creature lumbered within the forest. It had two heads and four sets of deviant eyes in the front and the back of its head. It's face bared ravenous fangs. It was accompanied by a small pack of hungry wolves.

Addison was climbing back down, when the branch he was hanging on broke away from the tree; he fell a few feet from the ground and the branch hit him in the face. Blood was dripping from the tree where the branch had broken off. Addison wiped his forehead and discovered that the tree was bleeding and not him. "That's odd," he said. "That's really freaky," Abigail responded. Athens reached for Addison's hand and helped him to his feet. "We need to leave this place before those creatures get any nearer! Let's head to the river and swim downstream, Its just beyond that circle of trees," Addison said as he pointed in the direction to the river.

"They're coming for you; You must hide!" Eliza hurried them along and waved her hands creating an invisible barrier.

They fled to the riverbank hoping nothing could follow their scent, but the river looked as if it was covered with shiny sheets of glass that sparkled like crystal. Downstream, there were twelve stepping-stones laid across the water. If they were too hasty, they could easily slip and fall. Addison stared at the stones. *What were they supposed to do?*

He squeezed his eyes shut for a minute, then opened them. "We need to Trust God to protect us. Let's give it a try!" Addison said as he moved forward, but then Abigail hurried ahead and called, "I'll go first." When Abigail jumped across the stones, she lost her balance and slipped, plunging into the icy cold river. The current pulled her downstream.

Athens had no choice but to go after her, so he dove in and swam as fast as he could. He noticed a long piece of driftwood floating a few feet away. Swimming against the tide, he grabbed ahold of it and kicked his feet, propelling himself in Abigail's direction.

Abigail bobbed up and down in the icy cold water as Athens finally made it to her after what seemed to take forever, though it was a matter of minutes. Reaching for the driftwood, her fingers barely grasped it and Athens grabbed her hand and pulled her to it. "Hold on tight." Their lives hung in the balance yet their faith kept them afloat.

Athens was trying to figure out a way to get out of the dangerous, cold waters when he saw a broken-down wooden bridge up ahead. Holding on to the driftwood with one arm and paddling with the other, he began moving toward the bridge. The driftwood plowed directly into the edge of bridge and teetered back and forth between two of the wooden posts before it came to a jolting stop.

As the strong current began pulling them away from the bridge, Athens grabbed ahold of one of the posts and pulled himself out. Then Abigail let go of the driftwood and pulled herself onto some timbers before stepping onto Athens' back to climb out of the water. Addison and Eliza followed along the riverbank and crossed to the other side of the river by the bridge. Natalie flew overhead to meet them.

Athens and Abigail lay on the riverbank to catch their breath. Minutes later, Addison and Eliza caught up to them.

"I'm so glad you guys are okay. I think it will be a miracle if we make it to Israel in one piece," Addison said as he bent down to his knees.

Athens raised his head to speak, but instead pointed. All turned their heads to a sparkling waterfall of enormous size and splendor just beyond the trees. In a clear pool at the bottom of the waterfall, something glistened in the sun's light.

Athens stood on shaky legs and gaped in awe for a moment, before he began approaching it. The others followed him. Out of thin air, the hands of God appeared and separated the crystal-clear waters into two. When they reached the waterfall, Athens saw that a magnificent sword was at the bottom of the pool which was what they had seen glistening in the distance. Athens walked through the narrow parting of the waters on the dry stones at the bottom of the pool. The cool water gently splashed his face as he reached for the sword; goosebumps covered his body as he graciously accepted the Sword of the Spirit. He felt an anointing power come over him as his hand rested on the sword.

Abigail, Natalie, and Addison stared in awe until the hands of God began to fade, dissolving into the waters and vanished. They had all witnessed the outpouring of the Holy Spirit and were filled with awe.

As Athens carried the sword back to his friends, the waters of the pool merged together once again, after he reached the bank. His chest rose and fell. Their mission was nearly complete. He led them back to the rock to prepare for their final destination. They linked arms for the last time as he spoke the words, "Guide me in Your truth and teach me Your ways, oh Lord, for You are my God, my Savior, my hope is in You all day long!"

In the twinkling of an eye, a strong breeze blew in and took them away.

CHAPTER 7

The King's Mansion

THE FINAL TRIUMPH

Jerusalem, Israel

Breathless and excited, Athens and his friends appeared in Israel like a whirlwind, wearing robust yet simple garments to keep them cool. Athens took in a breath of humid desert air, then glanced down at his apparel. His sandals were fitted on his feet and the Belt of Truth was secured around his waist. Abigail wore a beautiful, dark-blue scarf around her head; she was sure to blend in with the others.

"You look pretty, Abigail," Addison said smiling.

"Thank you. You never know who you might meet." She felt the silky scarf between her fingers when the wind moved it across her face. "I wonder when Eliza will be joining us," she said.

Athens wiped the sweat off his brow. If only he could sit down to rest for a moment underneath a nice shady tree;

his brain crawled with exhaustion, but there was no time to waste. They needed to get to the King's mansion.

Without a cloud in the sky, Addison and Natalie looked around but couldn't see anything past the sand dunes. Meanwhile, Athens and Abigail dropped to their knees in the scorching hot sand with the sun directly on their heads.

Athens glanced at Abigail. "We're almost done."

She gave a meek nod and rubbed her temples. "I'm starting to miss home. Aren't you?"

"Yeah, just a little." Athens lifted his eyes and began to pray, asking Jesus to bring a shade of hope. In an instant, a strong breeze breathed by. Some debris on the ground began moving upward in a spiraling motion, twirling around right next to them. It moved faster and faster until a beautiful Palm tree sprang forth from it that was large enough for the two of them to sit beneath and cool off. Athens slumped over in the sand, and Abigail nearly fainted against the tree trunk.

Addison walked over to stand beneath the tree when a coconut fell from the treetop and hit him on the head, and then cracked open. "Ouch, what the heck was that?" Addison rubbed his sore head and felt something wet dripping from his forehead. "Am I bleeding?" he looked down at his hands expecting to see blood, but it was only coconut milk.

"Oh don't be such a big baby." Giggling, Abigail reached for the coconut and broke it all the way open. "Any left for me? Coconut milk is my favorite," she added.

"Can I have some too please?" Natalie tweeted.

"God is good," Athens said while looking up into the palm branches.

"Yeah, He is," Addison grimaced, still rubbing his sore, wet, sticky head.

"Sorry for laughing, but you looked so funny when the coconut landed on your head." Abigail covered her mouth.

"It's fine," Addison chuckled while wiping the milk off his hands.

Breathing a sigh of relief, Athens mustered up the energy to stand on his feet. They needed to keep moving. As he stood, Athens caught sight of a man with three donkeys walking toward them.

"These donkeys are for you. They will take you where you need to go," the stranger said.

"Thank you, friend." Athens approached one of the donkeys and stroked its back. All of the donkeys had the shape of a cross woven into the hair on their backs. What did this mean? Athens was about to ask, but the man vanished into thin air.

Athens' chest swelled with gratitude. The donkeys were surely a gift from God, and were just what they needed to get them to Jerusalem.

Like a beam of light, Eliza appeared, waving her hands above her head as if trying to get their attention. When she saw the donkeys, she immediately bowed and said, "Shalom." She rubbed the neck of one of the donkeys, then straightened her back and turned her attention to Athens, Abigail, and Addison. "According to history, these donkeys are just like the one that Jesus rode when He went into Jerusalem. This is how the donkeys inherited their name, the Jerusalem donkey. Everyone stood in the streets, watching and waving their palm branches to celebrate the King. They even placed their coats and palm branches on the ground for the King to ride across. After all, He was an extraordinary King, and they wanted to honor him as such."

"Kind of like rolling out the red carpet to honor someone for something they did," Abigail said.

"Exactly! Everyone shouted, 'Hosanna, Hosanna! Praise the King of the Jews!' as Christ rode through town on the donkey. Every year, right before Easter, many people around the world celebrate this incredible event called Palm Sunday. Legend has it that the donkey loved his master so much that when Jesus died on the cross, the donkey couldn't bear to leave Him. So, as the sun was setting at the end of the day, the cross cast a shadow on the donkey's back, marking him with a symbol in remembrance of his love for his King." Eliza went on to say that the Jerusalem donkeys were, in fact, sent by God and would indeed carry them into the town of Bethlehem where they would find a place to stop for food and water before heading to the Old City of Jerusalem.

"Let's get going," Athens snapped his finger in the air like a prince and then climbed on one of the donkey's backs.

"Why are we going to Bethlehem first?" Abigail asked.

"To visit the town where Jesus was born, of course!" Eliza answered.

Abigail tried to get on the donkey but fell to one side and landed on her head with her arms and legs dangling beside her—a silly, awkward position, while Athens stifled a giggle. "Come on Abigail, you can do it," Natalie twittered.

Using a higher leap than before, Abigail finally turned around, got it right, and grabbed hold of the reins.

"Struggle much?" Athens smirked.

She glared at him and lifted her chin. "I've never ridden on a donkey before and quit honestly, I never want to ride on one again if I have anything to say about it." Addison sat back and watched while sitting on his donkey.

After ridding a short distance they came across a man pushing a large cart that was filled with over a hundred loaves of bread.

"Where do you think he's going with all that bread?" Abigail asked.

"Probably to the marketplace in Bethlehem," Athens replied.

As soon as they entered the city, they got off their donkeys to walk over to a well, where they met a lovely woman with olive skin and dark wavy hair filling a water vessel. She smiled as Athens walked by and inquired of him, "Are you here to meet the King?"

"Which king are you referring to?" Athens asked.

She lowered her head and whispered in his ear, "Why, the King of kings of course."

"We are; how did you know?" Athens waited for her to respond. He looked up into the sky and saw a white dove passing over their heads.

"A little bird told me," she answered. As she walked away, whispering, "Shalom, peace be with you."

Athens smiled and replied, "Shalom." As he turned back to the well, he noticed that her vessel sat on the ledge, full of water. "Wait!" Athens dashed over and picked it up, but when he turned around, she was already gone.

"Another mystery," he whispered under his breath.

The man carrying the loaves of bread passed through an archway covered with delicate, sweet grapevines that dangled from above. The man parked his cart near a two-story building surrounded by Palm trees.

Addison licked his lips. He could almost taste the freshness of the bread as the aroma lingered beneath their noses.

The man turned to face his cart, and Athens noticed his shirt had writing on it. The man's shirt read, *Bethlehem: The House of Bread.* "Interesting isn't it," he said.

"I'd love to have some myself, right now," Addison replied. "Me too," Natalie twittered.

A young woman sat down outdoors at one of the eateries, cradling her newborn baby as she waited to be served. She gently stroked her baby's cheek while softly singing a lullaby.

Twelve men were also waiting to be seated. "Who do you think those men are?" Addison asked.

"I don't know, but let's see if we can join them," Athens had a gut feeling he was supposed to meet them.

"No, no," Abigail said. "I don't want to bother them. Why don't you go ahead, and I'll go over and check on the donkeys in the stables; they may be hungry."

"Okay. I suppose we'll meet back up with you later," Athens confirmed, and off they went.

Just as Athens and Addison passed the archway to where the twelve men were standing, a strong breeze blew through the archway with them. It was as if the Spirit of God was speeding them on. All eyes turned to Athens and his friends.

Athens was the first to introduce himself. The men kindly invited Athens and his friends to join their company for a meal at the inn. He was happy to be invited to sit at their table, and realized that meeting them was no coincidence, but a divine appointment. God put them in the right place at just the right time.

A menorah sat on each of the long, white, wooden tables furnished with a warm basket of bread, a generous bowl of figs, nuts, and a fresh pitcher of water, as well as one chalice. As they all gathered to sit down, one of the men picked up the breadbasket and passed it around the table to share. He told them not to eat the bread until everyone held a piece in their hand. Next, he filled the chalice with the fruit of the vine, wine.

"Now," he said. "Everyone raise your piece of bread and give thanks to God for all your blessings, praising the name of the Lord—the King of kings!" He spoke further, saying that, "the bread represented the body, and the wine represented the blood of Jesus, God's only Son. He has the power to give life and to take it away. It is written that Jesus said to break bread in remembrance of Him; This is called communion."

Everyone nodded as they ate and drank to honor Christ for His mighty works, His mighty power and His everlasting love.

One of the disciples, got up to leave the table and stopped to ask Athens how much he would be willing to sell his donkey for, but Athens assured him the donkey was not for sale.

"Surely, you must have a price."

Again, Athens said, "No, I'm sorry, he's not for sale. I need him to take me to the Mount of Olives in Jerusalem."

"I'll pay you a great sum of money for him," the man insisted for a third time, as he tried to give Athens a bag of silver, but Athens' answer remained no. "What's so special about your donkey anyway?" he asked.

One of the other disciples got up and walked over to the balcony. "I see why you don't want to sell him. He's a very special donkey. That donkey came from the great city of Jerusalem." Athens got up and peered out the window.

Simon, one of the disciples, went on to say that a prophet named Micah, who was also a man of God, predicted seven hundred-fifty years before Christ that a Messiah would be born in Bethlehem, which means *House of Bread*. This Messiah would one day ride into town on a donkey and people would come to worship Him. They would call Him the King of the Jews. "This is the same breed of donkey."

Athens paced across the room as he listened.

Simon continued, "Not long after that, the people became fickle and betrayed Him, which led to His crucifixion and death on the cross. He was buried in a rich man's tomb and rose from His death after the third day. He stayed on earth for a time to empower His disciples and give them all spiritual gifts to carry out His work in Israel and throughout all the world." Simon tossed a fig into the air and caught it with his mouth, then continued, "Jesus performed great miracles, including feeding multitudes of people when they didn't have enough food." One of the men handed Addison the breadbasket. "He healed the sick and gave sight to the blind. Jesus gave up His earthly life for everyone, so that we could someday live in heaven in one of His many mansions." The disciple lifted his hands into the air.

"He was an innocent King who was the Son of God and Son of Man." Simon turned to his friends and smiled. "Someday, all people—men, women, and children of every nation, every color, and every language—will stand before the throne of God; everyone will be held accountable for their actions. Many rewards and punishments will be given on that great day."

"Did you know that God has many names?" said another disciple. "The name Messiah in Hebrew means *Anointed One*. Elohim means *The Living God and The One True God!* Messiah is like a title, and Yeshua is the Hebrew name meaning *Jesus!*" Athens sat back down at the table.

Matthew, another disciple, wanted to share one of his stories so everyone leaned in to listen. "One starry night, three kings of high esteem from the east traveled a great distance to the city of Bethlehem to meet a grand and glorious newborn King. According to scriptures, these three men followed the northern star to meet this magnificent child; they brought gifts of gold, frankincense, and myrrh in honor of the newborn King."

Matthew continued, "Shepherds tending their sheep out in the fields were visited by an angel of the Lord, named Gabriel, who told them not to be afraid and to follow the northern star to Bethlehem." He also added, "This happened more than two thousand years ago, and here we are today, still honoring Him and bringing glory to His name."

Athens walked over to the balcony to see the view. "That's an incredible story!" he said. We noticed the star of Bethlehem in the night sky while traveling here. He's an awesome King."

***

As Abigail carried water over to the donkeys and brought them a snack into the stables, she overheard one of them talking. Her mouth dropped open, "What do you know, these donkeys can talk too!" she exclaimed, though she was not particularly surprised.

One of the donkeys responded, "We only speak when we have something to say. For instance, when you tried to climb on my back, all we wanted to do was laugh!" one of them said as they all started laughing. "Hee-haw, hee-haw, hee-haw!"

Abigail shook her head and just looked at them with her hands on her hips. "Seriously! You try climbing on the back of something with four legs that's twice your size and see how that works out for you because it's definitely not easy!"

"But hey, it sure looked entertaining," said one of the donkeys as they continued laughing. "Hee-haw, hee-haw, hee-haw!"

"Some thanks I get for coming to take care of you." Abigail crossed her arms. "I think I'll go see what the boys are doing."

***

An hour later, Simon invited Athens and his friends to his house for dinner. Athens' stomach growled; he could hardly wait because they didn't end up eating much after receiving communion at the inn. They kindly accepted and were honored to be his guests.

Athens, Addison, Abigail, Natalie, and the three donkeys followed Simon to his home. Approaching his home they noticed a small garden filled with herbs and vegetables in his backyard. Athens' stomach began to growl again.

Simon's house was modestly decorated and had a delightful smell of incense that filled the atmosphere.

"Please feel free to get cleaned up before dinner; the washroom is down the hall and to the right," Simon mentioned.

There were clean linens hanging in the bathroom and fresh cut herbs sitting on the center of the kitchen table.

Three knocks rapped on the door. Simon welcomed eight more friends into his home. Two of the ladies who entered were sisters named Mary and Martha. Athens was inspired by Mary's devotion to God and enjoyed her company as they sat around the table and shared stories.

While eating stuffed grape leaves and seasoned pita bread, Athens explained that his journey had shown him the depths of the Father's love and helped him to understand who He is and who Jesus is. "Jesus is the Son of God our Father.

His commandments are the same yesterday, today, and forever. He has gone to prepare a place for us in His kingdom."

"Amen!" Matthew shouted he had also been invited to Simon's house.

After dinner, they pulled out their musical instruments and sang; they played a new song of praise, Giving glory to the King of Kings.

Before leaving, Athens, Abigail, and Addison thanked Simon and his company for their hospitality.

"We look forward to seeing you again someday. Perhaps we will meet in one of the King's mansions." Simon said. "Perhaps you are right," Addison agreed as he shook his hand and said Shalom.

Traveling onward, Athens and his trio of friends approached a valley just before they passed through the Mount of Olives. Completely mesmerized, they stood in awe soaking it all in. Never could they have imagined a place with such beautiful rolling hills and luscious rows of vineyards. It left them all speechless.

Upon entering Jerusalem, the Great City of Old, two men stood on the roadside. One blasted a shofar [horn] to get the people's attention, and the other held out his hands shouting in the streets telling the people to repent.

Athens smiled. Surely, they must know King Elohim.

He stopped and got off his donkey.

One of the men opened his mouth and flames blew out of it. "Behold, there's a great danger that lies ahead of you. Beware the prince of the air, Lucifer, that great and dreadful beast; the red dragon having seven heads and ten horns plans to destroy you."

A lump formed in Athens' throat. Meeting the two men was no accident but was another divine appointment to give him words of wisdom and fair warning.

An angry mob approached from behind and started throwing sticks and stones at them. The two prophets told the mob to repent and turn away from their sins before it was too late. The two prophets came to share a message of repentance, repair and restoration.

One of them yelled at the mob and said, "The only way to get to heaven is by asking Jesus to come into your life. He is the Life, the Truth, and the only way to enter into the Kingdom of Heaven and receive the gift of Eternal Life."

God's prophets warned the people of the consequences of what would happen if they didn't stop rebelling against God and chasing after their idols, but no one listened. Their hearts were hardened. The people no longer cared about what was right or wrong; they would rather live in bondage for temporary pleasure than in freedom forever.

"What if we don't want to have eternal life?" someone from the mob shouted. "Yeah, what if we don't want to live forever?"

One of the prophets held up his hands and said, "Your left hand is your past and your right hand is your future;

you are standing in the middle. What will you do? Will you choose the right path and look to the future, or will you look to your past and remain in sin?"

Not wanting to listen anymore, the mob picked up more sticks and stones and tried to kill the two men of God, Athens, and his friends. One of the prophets once again blew flames from his mouth, disorienting the mob.

The clouds and sky turned dark above. A mystical purple mist fell upon them and covered the entire city. Athens covered his head with his shield and ran for cover.

"What's happening? I can't see a thing in this fog," Abigail cried as she fanned her hands back and forth trying to see through the fog.

"Is this a good thing or a bad thing?" bellowed Addison. "Is it toxic?" He covered his nose and mouth with his shirt.

Just then, Eliza appeared as a flash of light, urging Athens and his friends to run to a secret passage near one of the city gates. A sequence of seven angels dressed in white gathered across the sky; their wings were filled with piercing eyes like that of great eagles each carried a bowl of wrath.

Through the dark purple fog, Lucifer—the red dragon with seven heads and ten horns—swooped down and swiped away a third of the crowd of people with his tail. The creature then attacked the two prophets, killing them on the spot and leaving their dead bodies in the street for all to see. Those who were left of the crowd rejoiced with gladness over the deaths of the men of God and even exchanged gifts to celebrate.

A great horn sounded from heaven and the clouds parted. The mighty voice of God descended from above saying, "Come up here!"

The bodies of the two prophets arose to life from the street, and they stood upright then floated into the air. The mob trembled with their mouths hanging open as they witnessed the two men being taken up into heaven.

The voice of God called out, saying to the seven angels, "Go, and pour out your wrath."

Each angel carried a different bowl of wrath, equaling seven in all. The angels released a punishment onto the people for what they had done—immediately killing three thousand of them. Another third of the crowd cried in agony as boils and sores appeared on their skin. Locusts swarmed through the city, searching out crops to devour. Fires broke out everywhere. The people fell to their knees and lay on their faces, probably wishing for death, but death would not have them.

A foul creature crawled out of the sea and approached them. He spoke to the people who were left behind and called them out by name, choosing them for his own and promising to bring peace to the land.

"Do you see the pain that God has put you through?" The beast from the sea spoke. "I, on the other hand, will protect you. I can make you richer than you could ever imagine." The words rang true in their minds, but it was a lie.

The people were deceived and took the mark of the beast on their hand or on their forehead and were gathered together. The dragon came once again and scooped the people up with his giant talons and flew away. Their cries and screams echoed through the distance.

A tear slipped down Athens' cheek. It was too late. They'd never escape.

Before the dragon could come back, Eliza led Athens and his friends through an underground tunnel in the heart of Jerusalem. She called it Hezekiah's tunnel; this passage way leads under King David and King Solomon's palace, and through it flows a natural spring. Near the entrance of the tunnel, they found a secret storage room filled with armor and weapons. Abigail and Addison found gear that was suitable for them.

When they reached the end of the tunnel, they peered out in to an enormous courtyard which connected to a long bridge. At the other side of the bridge sat a masterful golden gate which led into the King's province. In this place lay the peaceful gardens and splendid mansions of the King and His subjects.

Athens' heart picked up speed. Did he dare try to cross the bridge now?

Just as Athens had pondered this thought, Lucifer swooped down from the clouds as if he'd been tracking them all along. He flew after Athens with open jaws.

Abigail stood ready in her armor waiting for a clear shot at the dragon, when Addison jumped in front of her and pushed Athens out of harm's way. In the confusion of battle, they held tightly to their weapons and shot several silver-tipped arrows at the dragon hoping to force him to retreat. The arrows exploded on impact, but missed the dragon's hideous heads.

Lucifer staggered to the ground, but shook it off and the stench of his flaming breath filled the air. He circled around Athens and his friends, regaining his stamina.

The red dragon snarled at them, with fury disfiguring his many faces.

Natalie spread her wings and soared into the sky, letting out a piercing screech.

While Natalie distracted the dragon, Athens prepared his stance. He was fully armored and equipped, having the Gospel Shoes of Peace tightened to his feet, the Belt of Truth fastened around his waist, the Breastplate of Righteousness secured upon his chest, and the Helmet of Salvation set upon his head. He swiftly drew the Sword of the Spirit from his side and raised the Shield of Faith, standing his ground and ready to block the fiery darts of the evil one.

The dragon swept down, stretching all seven heads in Athens' direction.

Athens swung around with all his might and dealt the dragon a mighty blow, striking three of the dragon's heads all at once. The creature faltered to the ground and the angels eagerly watched.

Everyone outside the city gates heard the host of angels begin to cheer. "The dragon is slain!" they shouted.

Abigail's jaw dropped open as she witnessed the multitude of angels appearing in the clouds. She smiled in awe and pointed into the air above their heads.

Athens stepped onto the bridge and the cherubim signaled for the gates to open as the angels blasted their trumpets. The doors of the golden gate parted, and a great light shone through. From the mighty gate, a great company of princes, knights, and gentlemen of arms proceeded, and after them strode forth King Elohim in majesty. Athens watched in awe.

Without notice, the wicked red dragon began moving and rose to his feet. The serpent summoned his detestable creatures from the abyss to join him.

As Athens saw this, he took a firm stance for the battle was not yet over. Athens lifted his hands toward heaven and lightning fell from the sky, shaking the whole earth. A legion of angels bolted down from heaven on white horses, armed and ready to do battle with the dragon's demons. Another four creatures, more fearsome than the others, rose from the abyss. Each one had four heads and teeth like steel daggers, with great and terrible wings. The look of death was in their eyes as they waged war against the angels.

King Elohim called out to the valiant angelic creatures of the world, and mighty winds from the four corners of the earth sped their way. Spreading their wings wide and soaring through the air, each with enormous heads like lions, with teeth of ivory and four sets of piercing eyes like that of great eagles. They dispersed across the sky and enclosed upon the foul creatures.

The demons launched an attack and charged after Athens and his friends. Athens swiftly held up the Shield of Faith and a piercing wave of golden light exploded forth from him brighter than the sun. The demons were immediately incinerated and there was nothing left of them except for their ashes that were swept away by the wind. Flames dripped from Athens' body but he was not burned.

A colossal lightning bolt struck the ground and opened a huge crevice as deep as the earth's core, right outside the King's gates. The angels seized the wicked creatures and cast them down into the breach; an unbearable heat blazed from the great crevasse. The flames grew more intense still, as the demonic beings were cast into the pit.

Athens raised his sword and pointed to the dragon soaring in their midst. Without warning, a fierce bolt of lightning struck down from above and pierced the wing of the dragon like a spear. He plummeted to the earth near the opening of the rift.

King Elohim motioned from afar for Athens to deal the final blow. Athens advanced toward the dragon with adrenaline rushing through his blood. Though injured, the wrath of the dragon was deadly. Athens fought the dragon bravely and when Athens' strength was nearly spent, he found an opening to thrust the Sword of The Spirit into the chest of the wicked beast with all his might. Athens then looked to the King.

The sword seared in the heart of the dragon, and its corpse fell into the pit.

Blasts of trumpets and shouts of triumph sounded louder and louder from heaven above. *At last, the sound of victory!*

The golden harpists played their angelic tune. The cherubim sounded their horns once more.

All the angels were singing on-high as they descended from heaven. All praise to the King of Kings! For the dragon was cast into the pit...

Athens raised his hands in the air, praising God. "We did it!"

Abigail wrapped her arms around him and said, "I can't believe it!"

Addison gave a sinister laugh. "I've never seen anything like that in my entire life."

"Look!" Abigail pointed across the bridge.

King Elohim gestured at them to draw near, and they followed.

The King greeted Athens and his friends at the end of the bridge, standing just in front of the golden gate to His garden. "Take off your armor and remove your weapons; you have no further need of such things."

Athens obeyed; And they laid their armor and weapons at the King's feet. They wouldn't have to fight anymore since the enemy was vanquished.

King Elohim commanded one of His servants to bring forth a watering decanter from the well along with a white towel and the sacred oil of frankincense. The King then washed their feet, assuring them that it was necessary to wash away the dirt of the world before entering His kingdom.

"My beloved children, you have done very well indeed," King Elohim spoke to Athens, Abigail, and Addison. He ordered one of His servants to bring forth The Lamb's Book of Life.

The King then turned to the crowd of angels, princes, knights, and gentlemen of arms and announced, "Inside the golden book are the names of those who are privileged to access heaven. The golden book records all the faithful and loyal servants of God."

The words *Eternal Life* were embossed on top of the cover and began to glow when the King's fingertips passed over them.

King Elohim opened the cover and all ears could hear the words being sung, "Holy, Holy, Holy is the Lamb of God. Worthy is the King who does impossible things."

A brilliant bright light covered each name on every one of the pages as the King read them; including Athens, Abigail, and Addison. Each name was marked with the date and time that sealed their lives forever.

Athens leaned forward, staring at his name. "Why is my birthday in the book, my King?"

"Since the beginning of time, My chosen prophets have kept close records of every generation. Every bloodline through the ages, including those whom Christ was descended from, are recorded on these scrolls. You are here with Me now because Jesus fulfilled every prophecy ever written about Him." The King kindly looked into Athens' eyes and continued, "Since you have accomplished your quest and have delivered all the armor pieces, there is only one thing left for me to do."

The King stepped aside to reveal Athens' family and friends, who were waiting amongst the crowd of believers.

Athens gasped. His eyes grew wide as his chest rose with great joy.

"Now, you are an heir to My throne, a true prince. Wearing the armor gave you strength and courage, but now that you're here, you will be robed in white and wear a crown of victory. I have chosen you, and you have been adopted as an heir to My kingdom."

From the King's garden, The King and His company along with Athens and his friends, traveled to the King's mansion and gathered in the great hall for an unforgettable feast.

Eliza handed King Elohim the most masterfully crafted and elegant sword that anyone had ever seen. It must have been forged in the heavenly realms.

The King raised it over His head for everyone to see. The shine from the mirrored blade gave off a radiant glow from heaven. Everyone stared as they stood at attention.

"Now kneel," said the King.

Athens got down on one knee and bowed his head.

The mighty and powerful King tapped Athens on his right shoulder, then on his left shoulder, and lastly on the top of his head.

Then the King commanded, "Rise up as a true noble prince before your King."

Athens looked at the edge of the brilliantly polished sword and took note of the sharpness of the blade. The handle was made of ivory; the pommel was a Lion's head cast in gold with emerald eyes and sparkling teeth cut from diamonds.

A heavenly chorus of voices rang out and rejoiced as Athens rose to his feet, taking his rightful place as an heir to the King's throne.

Eliza bore a beautiful ring and a golden crown for King Elohim.

The King took the signet ring and slid it on to Athens' finger. It bore an inscription which read, *I Am that I Am, I'm the Lion, I'm the Lamb.* "A gift from your King," said Elohim.

Next, the King placed a crown upon Athens' head; It was a circlet of gold adorned with many leaves of gold.

After Athens was crowned, Abigail and Addison took their places next to Athens in King Elohim's Eternal Kingdom.

Athens stood in awe, "Thank you for allowing us to become a part of your kingdom." As he spoke, every knee was bent, and every head was bowed, giving God great glory for all He had done.

The King continued, "I have crowned you with victory over your enemies. You and your friends have proven to be trustworthy, faithful, and courageous. We have long prepared for such a time as this. A grand celebration and royal feast will be our blessing and last for seven years. Let the feast begin!" exclaimed the King, opening up his hands to the crowd of true believers. The entire host roared with the sound of clapping as their voices cheered with everlasting joy.

Athens leaned against a column and looked up into heaven through the open ceiling. The stars were so numerous that he couldn't count them all. The Kingdom of God would be forever expanding. There was no need to ever worry or doubt again, for their names had been written in the Lamb's Book of Life and would remain forever and ever until the very end of the age.

Armor of God—Life Application

Belt of Truth

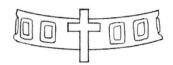

Ephesians 6:14 Stand firm then, with the belt of truth around your waist.
What is the belt of truth?
Who has the truth on their side?

The belt of Truth is believing in God's word, to be the whole Truth through Jesus Christ. He's our reference point for right and wrong. The Bible was written to share the Truth in its entirety. The Bible contains historical facts and records that have been proven over and over again. Not just part of it is true to suit our own needs, but all of it is True. Believers of Jesus Christ are Christians who Trust and believe His word to be the Truth, the Whole Truth, and nothing but the Truth. People who tell the Truth about God's mighty word have the Truth on their side.

John 14:6 NIV
Jesus said I am the way, the truth, and the life; no man comes to the Father except through me.

Psalms 25:5 NIV
Guide me in your truth and teach me, for you are God my Savior, and my hope is in you all day long.

Life Application:

We must always be truthful in all that we say and do so that we can walk upright, holding our heads up high, knowing we have the truth on our side, presenting ourselves blameless before God. Lies cause us to have a guilty conscience and can hurt us in the long run. It affects our relationship we have with God and others. By telling the truth, we are righteous in Christ. If God is for us, who can stand against us?

John 3:18 AMPC
He who trusts and believes in Him is Not judged, for there is no rejection, but he who doesn't believe is judged already because he has not trusted and believed in the trusted name of the only begotten son of God.

John 8:31 NIV
If you hold to my teachings, you are really my disciples. Then you will know the truth, and the truth will set you free.

2 Timothy 2:15 NIV
Do your best to present yourself to God as one approved, a workman who does not need to be ashamed and who correctly handles the word of truth.

2 Timothy 3:16 NLT
All Scripture is inspired by God and is useful to teach us what is true and to make us realize what is wrong in our lives. It corrects us when we are wrong and teaches us to do what is right.

Psalm 109:19 NIV
Let it be to him as a garment with which he covers himself,
And for a belt with which he constantly girds himself.

Prayer:

Lord Jesus, have mercy on me. Please help me to know the truth, show me the truth, so I can understand your will and your ways. Open my spiritual eyes so that I will confess the truth with my mouth. Please help me to always tell the truth even when I don't want to so that I can be trustworthy and full of honor. Thank you for being here for me and for your patience with me and loving me even when I don't deserve it. Guide me in your truth and teach me your ways, for you are my God, my Savior and my hope is in you all day long.

In Jesus' mighty name, Amen.

Breastplate of Righteousness

Ephesians 6:14
Stand firm then, with the breastplate of
righteousness in place.

What is the Breastplate of Righteousness?
Who is Righteous?

We must wear the breastplate to protect our heart. Our heart can be
easily wounded and deceived if we aren't guarding it.
Righteousness means to be right with God by choosing to do the right
thing. Those who stand strong in faith and do good are made
righteous through Jesus, for there are none righteous. Only God makes
us righteous. We can never be righteous without him.

Psalms 119:137 NIV
Righteous are you, Oh Lord, and your laws are right.
The statutes you have laid down are righteous.
They are fully trustworthy.

1 John 3:7 NIV
Dear children, do not let anyone lead you astray. He who does what is
right is righteous. He who does what is wrong is of the devil because
the devil has been sinning from the beginning.

Life Application:

In all things, we should do the right thing even when we don't feel like
it. We have to put ourselves in other people's shoes and ask ourselves
if what we are doing is what we would want someone to do to us. The
rewards are much greater than the punishment we will cause for
ourselves later. Sometimes the rewards for doing the right thing may
have to wait and that's okay, just remember that God is faithful to His
promises and is always watching over us. He will reward us in His
perfect time. He is always Righteous and worthy of our praise.

Matthew 5:6 & 10 NIV

Blessed are those who hunger and thirst for righteousness, for they will be filled. Blessed are those who are persecuted because of righteousness, for theirs is the kingdom of heaven.

Matthew 13:49 NIV

This is how it will be at the end of the age. The angels will come and separate the wicked from the righteous and throw them into the fiery furnace.

Philippians 3:9 NLT

I no longer count on my own righteousness through obeying the law; rather, I become righteous through faith in Christ. For God's way of making us right with himself depends on faith.

Romans 5:19 NLT

Because one person disobeyed God, many became sinners. But because one other person obeyed God, many will be made righteous.

Romans 13:12 NKJ

The night is almost gone, and the day is near. Therefore let us lay aside the deeds of darkness and put on the armor of light.

Prayer:

Lord Jesus, please forgive me of my sins. Cleanse me and transform my mind and heart. Fill me with Your Holy Spirit. Please help me to make the right choices and strengthen my heart and mind to do good things that are pleasing to you. Help me love others even when I don't feel like it so that I will be righteous in your sight. Help me to be faithfully and to serve you in all that I hear, think, see, say, and do. Thank you for guarding and protecting me when I need it. Thank you for walking with me through hard times and for choosing me to be your heir, your adopted child, whom you love.

In Jesus' mighty name, Amen.

Gospel Shoes of Peace

Ephesians 6:15 And with your feet fitted with the readiness that comes from the gospel of peace.

What are the Gospel shoes?
Who can wear them?

Christians wear the gospel shoes of peace to deliver God's message. We take the word of God by faith and share His word with others by spreading the good news of Jesus Christ to everyone, with thanksgiving and peace in our hearts! When we hear God's word, read God's word, study His word, memorize His word and pray. It helps us to know Him richly and gives us the spiritual food needed to share Him with confidence.

The Great commandment ~ Matthew 22:37 NIV
"Love the Lord your God with all your heart, and with all your soul and with all your mind. This is the first and greatest commandment. The second is like it: Love your neighbor as yourself.

The Great Commission ~ Matthew 28:19-20 NIV
Go and make disciples of all nations, baptizing them in the name of the Father, Son, and Holy Spirit and teaching them to obey everything I have commanded you. Surely, I am with you always, till the very end of the age.

Life Application

We should share the love of Jesus with our family and friends or anyone else that God puts in our lives and not be ashamed. Trusting Jesus to guide our footsteps is crucial so that we will not stumble or cause others to stumble and fall. Walk-in peace and in love. Encourage others to do the right thing too. Once Jesus comes into our lives, and fills our heart with his love, we should honor him by publicly being baptized by water just as Jesus did, to celebrate our new life as believers and to show our commitment to Him. It's important to be connected through God's word and to fellowship with other Christians. Try going to church and volunteering to help others. Take communion regularly. Always persevere and know that you are deeply loved.

Matthew 5:9 ASV
Blessed are the peacemakers, for they shall be called the sons of God.

Psalms 119:105 NIV
Your word is a lamp unto my feet and a light unto my path.

Galatians 5:22 NLT
But the Holy Spirit produces this kind of fruit in our lives: love, joy, peace, patience, kindness, goodness, faithfulness.

Philippians 4:4-6 NIV
Do not be anxious about anything, but in every situation, by prayer and petition, with thanksgiving, present your requests to God. And the peace of God, which surpasses all understanding will guard your heart and your mind in Christ Jesus.

Romans 14:19 CEB
So let's strive for the things that bring peace and the things that build each other up.

Numbers 6:26 NLT
May the Lord show you his favor and give you his peace.

Prayer

Lord Jesus, give me the strength and courage to go out into the world and spread the good news. Let your words be a lamp unto my feet and a light unto my path. Teach me to speak and act more like You. Grant me the wisdom and understanding I need so that I can forgive anyone who hurts me. Please give me peace in my heart that only you can give and help me to do the best that I can. May your light and blessings shine upon me and fill my life with your hope, love and peace so that I can be like a light to lead others to you.

In Jesus' mighty name, Amen!

Shield of Faith

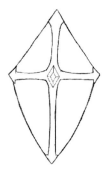

Ephesians 6:16
Take up the shield of faith with which you can extinguish all the flaming arrows of the evil one.

What is the shield of faith?
Why do I need it?

Faith is something we hope for but can not see. Faith is believing that God exists even though we can't see Him in person. The shield of faith protects us from Satan and his army. If we need more faith, we can ask Jesus for it. Satan will try to get us to do the wrong things. If we aren't careful, we will easily find ourselves going down the wrong path leading to sin. We cannot stand against Satan on our own; he is too powerful. Only by the power and blood of Jesus can we overcome the evil ones.

2 Samuel 22:31-32 NIV
As for God, his way is perfect; the word of the Lord is flawless. He is a shield for all to take refuge in him. For who is God besides the Lord? And who is the rock except for our God?

1 John 5:4 NIV
For everyone born of God overcomes the world. This is the victory that has overcome the world, even our faith. Who is it that overcomes the world? Only he who believes that Jesus is the son of God.

Life Application:

Faith is a gift; if we want more of it, we need to pray and ask Jesus to grant it to us so that our faith will grow stronger. We must have faith that God will protect us and provide for all of our needs. We often have to take a step of faith first to see God move in our lives.

Matthew 7:7 NIV
Jesus says, "Ask, and it will be given, seek, and you shall find, knock, and the door will be opened."

150

Hebrews 11:1 KJV
Now faith is the substance of things hoped for, the evidence of things not seen.

Matthew 17:20 NIV
If you have faith as small as a mustard seed, you can say to this mountain, move from here to there, and it will move. Nothing will be impossible for you.

Mark 4:30 NIV
The kingdom of God is described as a mustard seed, which is the smallest seed you plant in the ground. Yet when planted, it grows and becomes the largest of all garden plants, with such big branches that birds can perch in its shade.

Hebrew 11:6 NIV
And without faith it is impossible to please God, because anyone who comes to him must believe that he exists and that he rewards those who earnestly seek him.

Romans 10:9 NIV
If you declare with your mouth, "Jesus is Lord," and believe in your heart that God raised him from the dead, you'll be saved.

1Corinthians 16:13-14 NIV
Be on your guard, stand firm in the faith, be people of courage, be strong. Do everything in love.

Prayer:

Heavenly Father, you are my shield, my armor, my all in all. Thank you for sending your son Jesus to die on the cross for me and for allowing me to come before you to make my requests known. I ask that you strengthen my faith, bless my family and friends and protect us from harm's way. Send your guardian angels to guide my footsteps in the path that I am to go. Thank you for giving me more faith and courage. Thank you for forgiving me and my family of our sins. Thank you for your faithfulness and ever lasting love.

In Jesus' mighty name, Amen.

Helmet of Salvation

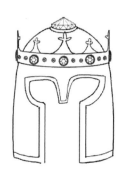

Ephesians 6:17
Take up the helmet of salvation and the sword
of the spirit, which is the word of God.

What is salvation? Where does it come from?
How do I get it?

Salvation is a free gift of eternal life, and salvation comes directly from God alone. God sent his only son to die for us so that we can have eternal life with Him. It is by grace; we are saved. We can't earn it. We get it by believing and trusting in God's mighty word. The only time God gives us permission to question Him is when we are discovering who He is. Ask Him to reveal Himself to you if you don't already know Him. Find a Bible or a person of true faith and dig into His word to search out the truth.

John 3:16 NIV
For God so loved the world that he gave his only begotten son so that whosoever believes in him should not perish but have eternal life.

Acts 4:12
Neither is there salvation in any other: for there is no other name under heaven given unto men by which we must be saved.

Life Application:

In order to enter heaven, we must truly believe that God is who He says He is. He is the creator of the heavens and the earth. He is the Alpha and Omega, the Beginning and the End. His words are the same yesterday, today, and forever. By believing and trusting in God, we carry faith in our hearts, praising Jesus as our Lord and Savior. Jesus freed us from our debt of sin. We must guard our hearts, minds, and thoughts against any wrong thinking that will cause us to keep sinning. When we turn away from sin, we become blameless.

Psalms 62:1 NIV
My soul finds rest in God alone; my salvation comes from him.
He alone is my rock and my salvation. He is my fortress. I will never be shaken.

Isaiah 59:17 NIV
He put on righteousness as his breastplate and the helmet of salvation on his head; he put on the garments of vengeance and wrapped himself in zeal as in a cloak.

Romans: 12:2 NIV
Do not conform any longer to the patterns of this world, but be transformed by the renewing of your mind. Then you will be able to attest and approve what God's will is, his good, pleasing, and perfect will.

1 Peter 1:13-15 NLT
Prepare your mind for action and exercise self control. Put all your hope in the gracious salvation that will come to you when Jesus Christ is revealed to the world. So you must live as Christ's obedient children. Don't slip back to your old ways of living to satisfy your own desire. You didn't know any better then...

1John 4:4 KJV
You are of God, little children, and have overcome them: because greater is he that is in you than he that is in the world.

Prayer:

Lord Jesus, I know that I am a sinner. Please forgive me for all of my sins and give me a clear understanding of how I can honor you. Please help me to know the plans that you have for me and help me to be a good example for others to follow. Fill me with the power of your love, grace, and forgiveness so that I can be a light in the world to encourage others to follow you, to do good and not evil. Thank you for being my savior, my salvation, and my all in all. Thank you for adopting me into your family and for granting me the gift of eternal life to be with you in heaven, forever.

In Jesus' mighty name, Amen.

Sword of the Spirit

Ephesians 6:18
Pray in the spirit on all occasions with all kinds of prayers and requests. Be alert and always keep on praying.

What is the sword of the spirit? How does it work?

The Sword of the Spirit is God's word. We must learn to use God's word correctly and protect it with all our hearts. We also need to guard our words so that they do not hurt others. Instead, let's use our words to build others up and encourage those around us who need comforted. We can speak life or death with the power of our tongues. God wants us to know Him personally, and He wants us to know ourselves as well as He knows us! We can know in our hearts that the spirit of God lives in us by what we say and do. We must learn to plant His word in our mind and our heart so when the time calls for it, we can defend God's mighty word.

<u>Romans 8:14 NIV</u>
Those who are led by the spirit of God are sons of God. For you did not receive a spirit that makes you a slave again to fear, but you received the spirit of sonship. And by him, we cry Abba Father. The spirit himself testifies with our spirit that we are God's children.

<u>2 Corinthians 10:3-4 NIV</u>
For though we live in the world, we do not wage war as the world does. The weapons we fight with are not the weapons of the world. On the contrary, they have divine power to demolish strongholds.

<u>Life Application:</u>

Our lives are like the seeds that are planted in this world. The seeds we produce can be good or bad. If properly cared for, then we will produce good fruits, and our seeds will prosper, but if we aren't careful with our words and actions, then our seeds won't produce good fruit but will wither and die.

Let's be productive and produce good fruit that pleases God. Let's stay connected to Jesus by talking to Him everyday through prayer. It's important to have fellowship with other believers who strengthen us. Reading the Bible daily will strengthen our heart and mind. Our words are like a two-edged sword! Iron sharpens iron, so must we learn to sharpen iron by what we say and do.

Matthew 10:32-34 NIV
Whosoever acknowledges me before men, I will also acknowledge him before my Father in heaven, but whoever disowns me before men, I will disown him before my Father in heaven. Do not suppose that I have come to bring peace to the earth, but a sword.

Acts 2:4 NIV
All of them were filled with the Holy Spirit and began to speak in other tongues as the Spirit enabled them.

Acts 4:31 NIV
After they prayed, the place where they were meeting was shaken. And they were all filled with the Holy Spirit and spoke the word of God boldly.

John 1:1
In the beginning was the word, and the word was with God, and the word was God.

Prayer:

Lord Jesus, thank you for all that you've done, for all that you are doing, and for what is yet to come. Please help me to control my tongue so that I will not sin against you by the things I say. Protect my mind, body, and soul against my enemies who wish me harm. Please give me the wisdom to speak the truth with confidence and boldness. Guard my thoughts against wanting to do the wrong things. Plant your seeds of love, hope, and faith in my heart so that they will prosper and grow, giving me the ability to share with others what you have freely given to me. I pray for your favor to be on my life and those around me.

In Jesus' mighty name, Amen.

Full Armor Verses

Ephesians 6:13-19
New English Translation

¹³ For this reason, take up the full armor of God so that you may be able to stand your ground on the evil day, and having done everything, to stand. ¹⁴ Stand firm therefore, by fastening the belt of truth around your waist, by putting on the breastplate of righteousness, ¹⁵ by fitting your feet with the preparation that comes from the good news of peace, ¹⁶ and in all of this, by taking up the shield of faith with which you can extinguish all the flaming arrows of the evil one. ¹⁷ And take the helmet of salvation and the sword of the Spirit (which is the word of God). ¹⁸ With every prayer and petition, pray at all times in the Spirit, and to this end be alert, with all perseverance and petitions for all the saints. ¹⁹ Pray for me also, that I may be given the right words when I begin to speak—that I may confidently make known the mystery of the gospel.

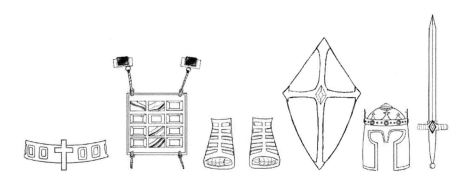

Fun Facts

Fun Facts: Chapter 1

- The description of Athens' room and how he got his name is true. He received the True-Blue Panther award in 8th grade at Pine View Middle school for being an exceptional student of the year. (Being thoughtful, courageous, excellent in his work and helpful to those around him).

- Genesis 1:1-31, 2:1 & 6:1-6 speaks of creation and the demigods.

- Peter 3:13-15 tells us that God will reward us for doing what is right.

- Athens loves forging with fire and making knives, blades, and axes. He's also learning how to make bows and arrows from trees that he's cut down. He has two shofar horns and many sacred oils from Israel. The horns are blown during feasts and festivals in Israel every year and the oils are used for anointing God's chosen ones.

- Athens has an Onyx globe trimmed in gold from Greece that was purchased before he was born and given to him for one of his birthdays.

- The exotic flowers around the well are real and look like monks before they blossom into doves. Page 19.

- In Athens' backyard on his Papaya tree are caterpillars with white crosses on their foreheads. See if you can find the small caterpillar in one of the pictures.

- Athens' middle name is Seth. It means a promise renewed. He is the third born of Adam, just like Seth in the Bible is the third born of Adam and Eve. Genesis 2:5-25 & Matthew 1:1. Jesus was born through the lineage of Seth.

- The Lamb's Book of Life exists, aka The Book of Life! In Daniel 12:1, Luke 10:20, Philippians 4:3, 20:15. Revelations 3:5, Revelations 20:15.

- *God's Trinity: His power starts in your mind: **The Father** and moves to your heart: **The Holy Spirit** then to your hands: **Jesus** Pg. 19*

Fun Facts: Chapter 2

- The Breastplate of Righteousness truly exists and was worn by the High Priests of Israel. Exod. 25:15.

- The Northern Star is the Star of Bethlehem and has reappeared after 2,000 years since Jesus' birth.

- The Resurrection plant, aka the Rose of Jericho blossoms, wherever it's at without being planted.

- The story of Athens and the dry bones in the valley was created from Ezekiel 37 in the Bible.

- The Valley of the Kings in Egypt is a touristy place.

The Golden Garments (8th) of the Kohen Gadol Shemot 28:4:42

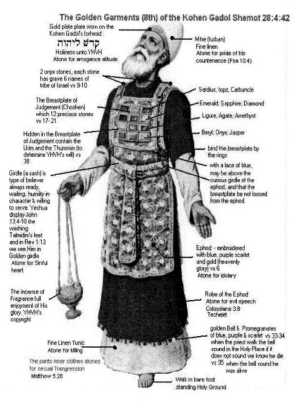

Gold plate plate worn on the Kohen Gadol's forhead:

קדש ליהוה

Holiness unto YHVH
Atone for arrogance attitude

2 onyx stones, each stone has grave 6 names of tribe of Israel vs 9-10

The Breastplate of Judgement (Choshen) which 12 precious stones vs 17-21

Hidden in the Breastplate of Judgement contain the Urim and the Thummim (to determine YHVH's will) vs 30

Girdle (a sash) is type of believer always ready, waiting, humility in character & willing to serve. Yeshua display John 13:4-10 the washing Talmidim's feet and in Rev 1:13 we see Him in Golden girdle Atone for Sinful heart

The incense of Fragrance full enjoyment of His glory. YHVH's copyright

Fine Linen Tunic Atone for killing

The pants inner clothes atones for sexual Transgression Matthew 5:28

Mitre (turban)
Fine linen
Atone for pride of his countenance (Psa 10:4)

Sardius; topz; Carbuncle
Emerald; Sapphire; Diamond
Ligure; Agate; Amethyst
Beryl; Onyx; Jasper

bind the breastplate by the rings

with a lace of blue, may be above the curious girdle of the ephod, and that the breastplate be not loosed from the ephod

Ephod: - embroidered with blue, purple scarlet and gold (heavenly glory) vs 6
Atone for idolary

Robe of the Ephod
Atone for evil speech
Colossians 3:8
Techelet

golden Bell & Promegranates of blue, purple & scarlet vs 33-34 when the priest walk the bell sound in the Holy Place if it does not sound we know he die vs 35 when the bell sound he was alive

Walk in bare foot standing Holy Ground

161

Fun Facts: Chapter 3

- Fiery tornados and dust devils really exist in different parts of the world, including Australia.

- The Gospel Shoes of Peace are what believers wear on their feet to share the Good News about Jesus.

- Male Peacock spiders are very cool and really dance to find a mate. They are the size of a grain of rice!

- People around the world live in Beehive homes.

- The tower of Babel is in the book of Genesis 11:1-9.

- Rainbow Eucalyptus trees are native to the Philippines but grow in other places worldwide.

- Manna rained down from heaven during the Israelites 40 years in the wilderness. After entering the Promise Land it stopped once they ate the food from the land.

- There really are trees that appears to bleed when cut. They are called Bloodwood, Dragon's blood or Wild Teak.

Fun Facts: Chapter 4

- The two cows with the number 7 on their heads are likened to the two cows in Pharaoh's dream from the Bible. One of the cows was born in Israel, and one was born in the United States on the same day, September 25th, 2014. See author Jonathan Cahn's story about their prophetic meaning (Feast and Famine).

- Sugar Loaf Mountain is in Brazil. Sugar beets supply most of their nation's sugar needs.

- 100-pound sized hailstones are mentioned in the last book of the Bible in Revelation 16:21.

- The four emblems on the shield have true meaning from the Bible. See Ezekiel 1:10 & Revelation 4:6.

- Athens really has a fear of heights. He prays, seeking God's favor, love, wisdom, and direction concerning all things in his daily walk with Christ.

- Christ The Redeemer is one of the seven wonders of the world located in Rio de Janeiro, Brazil.

- The Pastor at my church told a story and said, "Don't just keep the faith, share it."

Significance of the two Shemitah calves:
2. Represent 14 cows in Pharoah's dream

Fun Facts: Chapter 5

- Wolf Blood Moons and glow worms are super rare.

- Stones of Eilat are only found in King Solomon's Mine in Israel and can be purchased online.

- Deception Island is in Antarctica. The black hole really exists and keeps growing bigger; it keeps appearing and disappearing. It's believed that Nephillim use the black hole to travel through.

- The story about the secret remnant of Athens' hair is made up from Ezekiel 5:1-5 found in the Bible.

- The Crucifix catfish, also known as the Sail Catfish, is super cool. Athens has the one in the picture.

- The Aurora Borealis lights in Alaska are magnificent.

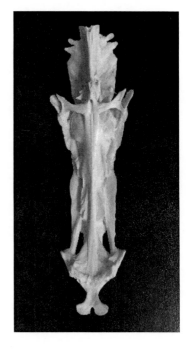

Fun Facts: Chapter 6

- Many languages are spoken in America because people travel from all over the world to live here. It's the home of the free and the brave. In God we trust is written on all the currency.

- The majestic sequoia redwood trees in California are the largest in the world and live longer than most. They can reach 367 feet tall and 22 feet wide and can produce 400,000 seeds per tree every year.

- The natural phenomenon at Bridal Veil Falls, California, occurs every year for two weeks at the end of February.

- The armor pieces are spiritual weapons Christians use to defeat spiritual enemies.

- Two types of Jesus moths exist in America. You may even spot one by accident.

- Jesus was baptized by John the Baptist in the Jordan River. God desires for us to be baptized by water once we become believers. Take a step of faith and follow Him. Athens is in the picture on the right, being baptized by Pastor Kelly from our church.

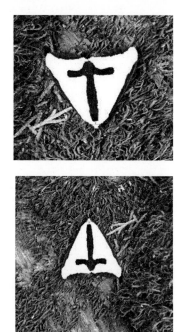

Fun Facts: Chapter 7

- Jerusalem/Jesus donkeys are real animals. My neighbor has two of them. A talking donkey is mentioned in the Bible ~ Numbers 22:21-41. Find out what happened.

- The purple mist really existed long ago near the Dead Sea in Israel and was very toxic.

- The meaning: four corners of the earth represent north, south, east, and west. Ancient scrolls exist and teach the lineage of Jesus going all the way back to the first man ever created, who was Adam.

- Christians take communion to keep their promise to God by honoring His Son Jesus, who said to eat of the bread and drink of the wine in remembrance of Him. He covered our sins with His life and shed His blood on the cross for us. Before taking communion, we must always ask for forgiveness of our sins first, so we remain blameless and full of His love, honor, and grace.

- The two prophets are mentioned in the last book of the Bible in Revelation. The picture of the man carrying the loaves of bread is from Jerusalem.

- B.C. means before Christ & A.D. means Anno Domini ~ In the year of our Lord. Not after death, as many people believe. Time revolves around the birth of Jesus. Our birthday stems from the birth of Christ. From today's date, roughly 2021 years ago, is when He walked the Earth.

- God told the Israelites to put the blood of a lamb on their doorposts during Passover in the Old Testament. Now we know this symbolizes the blood of Jesus, who came into the world to be the last living sacrifice for all sin. Throughout History lambs were born in Bethlehem and then sacrificed in Jerusalem for the sins of people just like Jesus was.

- The great red dragon Lucifer, aka the devil, was mentioned in the book of Revelation 12 in the Bible.

- The picture of Jesus' tomb in Israel was taken in July of 2018.

- The year 2020 was known as the year of the locust. In the Bible, it talks about locusts devouring everything in sight. Revelations 9:3.

- Dig deeper, look closer to uncover many cool things in the book that you can discover on your own.

- *Become a warrior for Jesus by getting involved. Here are ways for you to help; Pray for us, our mission and God's vision. Volunteer in some fashion to help spread the word or make a donation to help support our ministry to get our books and program into the hands of many people locally and worldwide.*

- *Consider becoming a partner to help keep this ministry alive, enabling us to have a global impact one youth at a time.*

- *Soon to come will be a program designed to teach kids how to suit up and put on the full armor of God, walking in peace and love, trusting in the name of Jesus!*

You may contact me via email: Adventureswithathens1@gmail.com

Is your name written in the Lamb's Book of Life?

Join the quest and sign up today!

adventureswithathens1@gmail.com

Learn how to become a warrior for Jesus and an heir to His everlasting kingdom!

This is where one story ends and a new adventure begins.

Help share the message of hope and love around the world by supporting this ministry. You will be helping to get this book and program into many hands and hearts of young people worldwide.

God Bless you as you partner with us to make a noble global impact. We can change lives one step at a time!

FOR MORE INFORMATION, PLEASE CONTACT ME BY EMAIL:

adventureswithathens1@gmail.com

Soon to come will be a complete guide with detailed information to go along with my new program for putting on the Full Armor of God. I can't wait to share it with you and watch lives be transformed by the anointing power of God!

My God Who is He

El Shaddai - (God Almighty), Elohim - (One True God),
Emmanuel (God with us), El Elyon - (Most High God),
Extraordinary, Exact, Exceptional, Essential, Ethical,
Eternal, Exemplified, Exalted, Equipped, Elevated,
Enlightened, Esteemed, Enriched, Engaged, Enraged,
Elated, Ecstatic, Empathetic, Exotic, Enthusiastic,
Exhorter, Energizer, Encourager, Excellent, Expert,
Eminent, Exuberant, Eloquent, Efficient, Earnest,
Everlasting, Edifying, Empowering, Exhilarating,
Endearing, Entertaining, Enduring, Elaborate,
Exquisite, Effective, Enjoyable, Endless.

He is my Everything and will never be Extinct!

Written By: Kem Arfaras

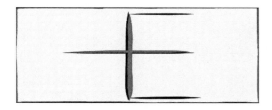

Missions Around the World

Preparing for Thailand

New Delhi, India

America ~ Israel ~ VBS

Local and Global Missions

About the Author

Kem's love for literary expression took root as an honored elementary school student whose poems were showcased in its periodical. She wrote her first short story at the age of ten and holds the only copy. Her heart strings are children. Kem is a wife,  sister, mother, aunt, and grandmother. She also loves photography and teaching the Word of God through scripture and personal life experiences. She's a missionary at heart and has traveled the globe making friends around the world. Kem has three children, four grandchildren, and a marriage of 35 years to a first-generation Greek American. In the midst of it all, her insatiable love for children still hadn't been pacified, so she opened a daycare and a preschool for many years while raising her own family in Florida. She taught Pre-K and Art from Pre-K through High School at Tampa Christian Community School while pursuing her life's crown jewel. She has spent much of her life ministering and volunteering in various places worldwide to help further the Kingdom of God. She's been chosen many times over to take part in leading several Vacation Bible School Programs globally, teaching the true anointing power of God's Word. It's her life dream to build settings around the world for putting on the full Armor of God, helping people of all ages come to know the true anointing power of God, while leading as many souls as possible to Jesus before leaving this great planet Earth.

Her literary style is intentionally magical, adventurous, and whimsical, leaving no rock unturned, it's sure to inspire and coerce the reader to embrace the timelessness that can only be found in an open book and in the open arms of one Godhead found in Jesus Christ. Her hope is to be as much of a blessing to you as He's been to her!

Journey-Wise –
Romans 12:2